TANGL...
ANIMA...

Elephant
Emergency

Zoe saw the edge of a tusk. A moment later, the doorway was filled by an elephant with its trunk curled up high and back so that it touched the top of the animal's head. Its mouth was open as though it was smiling and it glanced carefully left and right, taking everything in.

Zoe clenched her fists with excitement...

First published in the UK in 2017 by Usborne Publishing Ltd.,
Usborne House, 83-85 Saffron Hill, London EC1N 8RT, England.
www.usborne.com

Copyright © Tamsyn Murray, 2017

The right of Tamsyn Murray to be identified as the author
of this work has been asserted by her in accordance with the
Copyright, Designs and Patents Act, 1988.

Cover and inside illustrations by Jean Claude, Courtesy of Advocate Art,
and Chuck Groenink.
Illustrations copyright © Usborne Publishing Ltd., 2017

The name Usborne and the devices ⓠ ⊕ are Trade Marks of
Usborne Publishing Ltd.

This is a work of fiction. The characters, incidents, and dialogues are products of the
author's imagination and are not to be construed as real. Any resemblance to actual
events or persons, living or dead, is entirely coincidental.

A CIP catalogue record for this book is available from the British Library.

JFMAM JASOND/17

ISBN 9781474932011 04413/1

Printed in the UK.

Chapter One

"**W**e've got a problem."

Zoe Fox looked up from her homework to see Dad frowning down at his phone. It was seven-thirty on a Friday evening in October and she was sitting with her parents around a roaring fire in the living room of Tanglewood Manor. Her little brother, Rory, was fast asleep upstairs and the animals of Tanglewood were all safely tucked up for the night. Or were they?

Zoe felt a stab of worry. Tanglewood Animal Park was home to over 350 creatures, big and small – had one of them been hurt?

Mum stopped sketching her design for a giraffe habitat. "What is it?"

Dad's frown deepened. "How soon can you get the new elephant enclosure ready?"

Zoe blinked. Her mum had been working hard to design and oversee a large, brand-new elephant home right next door to Tanglewood's latest expansion, the Savannah Safari. But although the building work was complete, Zoe knew there was still a lot to be done before the habitat was elephant-ready.

"Why?" Mum asked, lowering her pencil. "What's happened?"

"I've just had an email from Pawprints Zoo. They've closed down and need to find an urgent home for their family of African elephants."

Zoe felt her eyes widen in shock. Zoos closed down for lots of reasons, from not enough visitors to worries about safety, but it was almost always bad news for the animals who lived there. Some of them would be easy to rehouse but others – like elephants – needed a strong, purpose-built enclosure with lots of space and ditches all around to keep them inside. It wouldn't be easy to find a home for every animal at Pawprints.

Mum shook her head. "I don't know – it's a bit sooner than I'd like. How many elephants do they have?"

"Six – two males and four females." Dad glanced at Zoe. "One of the girls is an infant – only four months old."

Zoe's insides danced with sudden excitement. What could be cuter than a baby elephant?

"Don't get carried away," Mum warned her. "We don't know if they're coming here yet. Isn't there anywhere else? We promised Berlin Zoo we'd take their herd, remember?"

Mr Fox checked his phone. "A few places have offered to take one or two but nowhere has room to take them all. And you know how close elephant families are – they don't like to be separated."

That's true, Zoe thought, remembering a documentary she'd seen where the presenters had talked about how deeply elephants felt things like love and friendship – they even cried sometimes. And most animals struggled when they went to a new zoo – Tanglewood's Sumatran tiger, Tindu, had taken a long time to settle in when he'd first arrived. The Pawprints elephants would find moving house even more difficult if they were apart.

"We can't take both herds," Dad went on. "And Pawprints needs our help most."

"How soon do they need to move?" Mum asked.

"Next week. I don't know the full story yet but it sounds like a real nightmare." He paused. "So what do you think? Could we be ready in time?"

Mum let out a long sigh and rubbed her face. "I don't think we have much choice. We can't let them become homeless, especially not with an infant in the herd."

"Yes!" Zoe squealed, filled with delight. "We're going to have a baby elephant! Oh, I can't wait to tell Oliver!"

Oliver was the son of Tanglewood's Chief Vet, Max, and he was the same age as Zoe. She reached for her phone to send him a message, knowing he'd be just as over the moon as she was at the news.

"Hold on, Zoe," Dad said. "It's not agreed yet. Moving six elephants is no easy task and a lot depends on their personalities. The elephant keeper at Pawprints has invited me and Max to visit him tomorrow – I'll know more then."

Zoe went very still. "Oh…can I come with you? It's Saturday so there's no school—"

"Zoe," Dad interrupted, his eyebrows beetling together into a frown. "I don't—"

"I promise I'll be good, you won't even know I am there," she gabbled, pretending not to hear him. "And Oliver could come too, that way I'll have someone to hang out with if you have things you need to do. Please, Dad."

She held her breath as her parents exchanged a look. Long seconds ticked by, then Dad tipped his head. "I'll need to speak to Max—"

"Yes!" Zoe clenched her hand into a triumphant fist.

"It might not be possible, Zoe," Mum said doubtfully. "It all depends what the situation is at Pawprints. Don't be disappointed if you can't go after all."

"If you do come, you'll need to be ready early," Dad said. "Make sure you get your Tanglewood animal duties out of the way first thing in the morning."

Zoe tapped at her phone with feverish fingers. "I will," she promised. "I'm setting an alarm for six-thirty tomorrow."

Dad announced he was going to call Max, leaving Zoe and her mum to finish their work. Zoe found it hard to concentrate and kept picturing the cutest little elephant calf wobbling around the elephant enclosure, its trunk curled around its mother's tail. It was very sad that they had to leave their home at Pawprints but Zoe couldn't help hoping they would be coming to Tanglewood, and from the sound of things, they might even arrive in time for her birthday, which was less than two weeks away. *Imagine our very own baby elephant,* Zoe thought, staring into the flickering flames of the fire. *Oh, please let it happen!*

The next morning, Zoe was up early. She dressed in a hurry and tugged her Tanglewood fleece over her head. Then she gulped down a bowl of cereal and let herself out of the back door to crunch along the gravel path that led to Tanglewood and its animals.

The sun wasn't even peeping over the horizon and the park's pathways were empty, but that didn't mean Zoe was alone; each leafy enclosure she passed had a fascinating animal inside, from wolves to wallabies. Tanglewood's main gates opened to visitors at nine-thirty but there was plenty to be done before then each morning. Zoe knew there would already be several keepers making their way around the park, taking food to their animals and pushing wheelbarrows to clean up any mess that had built up overnight. Gradually, the air became filled with the sounds of the park waking up – the ring-tailed lemurs squabbling, the gibbons whooping as they swung from rope to rope, and the mighty roar of Sinbad the lion reminding everyone he was in charge. *Business as usual*, Zoe thought, grinning to herself.

The guinea pigs were their usual chattering selves as Zoe set about cleaning their enclosures. They'd been one of the first animals she'd been able to get involved with when her family had bought Tanglewood and moved into the grand manor house in the centre of the park, and they were still among her favourites. She loved being able to stroke them, and she felt as if each animal was a little friend. She felt the same way about Flash, the baby zebra who'd been born not long after Zoe and her family had moved to the park, and she loved seeing him growing bigger and stronger. Tindu the tiger and Tanglewood's other big cats were breathtaking and magnificent but she'd never be able to get close enough to touch them. Would the new baby elephant be the same?

Once the guinea pigs were safely back in their freshly tidied enclosures, Zoe checked her watch. It was almost seven-thirty and she hadn't heard from her dad about where to meet him for the trip to Pawprints. She knew he was probably busy around the park but she couldn't help worrying that he might have changed his mind and gone without her.

Telling herself she was being silly, Zoe headed towards the elephant house. Work had been going on for weeks, and the finished building had heated floors and lots of natural light, plus a large grass and sand paddock outside filled with log piles and several water pools. The habitat was surrounded by deep ditches but there was a wide path which would allow the elephants to explore the fields that made up the new Savannah Safari, the entrance to which was nearby. The safari itself wasn't quite finished – it was still closed off with big wooden fences – but once everything was ready, visitors would ride on special buses and pass large paddocks designed to mimic the animals' habitat in the wild. Each bus would have an expert guide on board to explain what the public were seeing, and eventually there would be giraffes, rhinos and a herd of gazelles, all in their own fields. Zoe felt another thrill at the thought of even more new animals joining the Tanglewood family, but she was especially excited about the elephants.

She hurried underneath Snowy Point, where Tanglewood's pair of snow leopards lived, and down towards the meerkat enclosure. There were more keepers around now – Zoe waved as she saw Cassie heading towards the tiger house. She spotted a few members of the gardening team clearing up the crisp tawny leaves that had fallen in the night, but there was no sign of Zoe's dad or Max. Growing more and more fidgety as she walked, Zoe finally gave in and pulled out her phone.

Hey Dad, where are you?

Minutes ticked by. Impatient, Zoe decided to head home; maybe Dad was waiting for her there? She passed Abie, the red-panda keeper, who was on her way to give bamboo-loving Kushpu and Hardeep their breakfast, and grinned a greeting. Another time, Zoe might have stopped to help but this morning her head was filled with elephants.

Her phone buzzed as she walked. It was Dad.

Leaving for Pawprints in 30 minutes if you still want to come? Meet outside the manor.

Zoe let out a gasp of delight – if she still wanted to come? Of course she did! Stuffing her phone firmly into the pocket of her fleece, she started to run.

Chapter Two

The journey to Pawprints took an hour and a half. Zoe and Oliver sat in the back seat of the Tanglewood-emblazoned 4x4 and watched videos of elephants on Zoe's tablet as they whizzed along the motorway.

"Isn't it amazing they live for so long?" Oliver said, as a clip from a BBC documentary showed an elderly elephant leading a herd across some grasslands. "Seventy is a great age for a wild animal

– they must have seen everything by then. I suppose that's why the oldest elephant in a group is the one in charge."

"The oldest *girl* elephant," Zoe reminded him. "In the wild, the boys only stay with the herd until they're about fifteen – after that they go and live on their own. So groups like this one –" she pointed at the screen – "will be made up of adult females and their children. And the oldest one is the boss – she's called the matriarch."

Oliver nodded, his gaze glued to the tablet. "I like the way they all work together to take care of the younger ones. What do they call them again – is it 'aunties'?"

Max glanced over his shoulder. "That's right – elephants believe in sharing the childcare among the herd."

He smiled and Zoe wondered if he was thinking of the way everyone at Tanglewood had helped him to look after his son when Oliver's mother had died several years earlier. In some ways, Tanglewood is like a big family, Zoe thought warmly.

"But obviously things work a little differently in captivity," Max went on. "The group we're going to see today is mixed – we've got a matriarch, plus her daughter, who has a juvenile boy of around eight and an infant girl. Then there's an unrelated female – we'll call her a friend – and a fully mature bull elephant. He's the dad of the younger ones."

"A family," Zoe said, remembering her mother's description from the night before. "That's why it's so important to keep them together."

The video clip ended and Oliver glanced out of the window. "Look, there's a sign for Pawprints Zoo! We can't be far away now."

"Just a few more minutes," Zoe's dad confirmed, steering the car off the motorway. "Why don't you let the staff at Pawprints know we'll be arriving soon, Max?"

Zoe listened as Max spoke to someone called Joe. "He'll meet us at the entrance," Max said, once he'd rung off. He glanced back at Zoe and

Oliver. "I hope you're ready to make some new friends?"

Zoe felt a shiver run through her as she exchanged an eager look with Oliver. The excitement was about to go off the charts!

The main gates to Pawprints were locked with a thick, heavy-looking chain, but Zoe could see an old white van on the other side, with a man waiting next to it: Joe, she guessed. The gates weren't as imposing as the ones at Tanglewood, which had roaring stone lions keeping guard on each side. These gates looked old and they creaked in protest when the keeper hauled them open. Dad buzzed his window down.

"Hi, I'm Ben Fox. This is Max Chambers, Tanglewood's Chief Vet, plus Zoe and Oliver in the back. You must be Joe."

The man nodded. "Yes, I'm the elephant keeper here." He smiled at Zoe and Oliver. "Good to meet you all."

"Do you want to lead the way?" Zoe's dad asked.

"Of course," Joe said. "Follow my van. We'll park

in the car park and walk to the elephant house. There's no shortage of parking spaces."

He waited until Zoe's dad had driven the 4x4 through the gates, then locked them and climbed into his van. The road was full of potholes and bumps that Mr Fox did his best to avoid. When they reached the zoo itself, Zoe found it sad to see an almost-empty car park when she knew Tanglewood would be jammed with visitors. *The few cars that are here must belong to the keepers*, she thought, trying not to notice the litter blowing across the pitted tarmac and the faded signs pointing to the way in.

"It's all a bit neglected, isn't it?" Oliver murmured once they'd got out of the car.

Zoe knew what he meant. Tanglewood had felt the same when she'd first arrived, as though it needed some love and attention to bring it back to its glory. But as she got past the entrance kiosks, she could see that Pawprints needed a lot more than love; everywhere she looked, she saw enclosures that were damaged and in need of repair or fences that had been propped up with bits of metal and wood. The play area was closed off with red-and-white tape, and the ice-cream hut didn't look as though it had been open for a long time. Most of the animal habitats were empty. No wonder it had closed down: there was nothing for the visitors to see.

Joe seemed embarrassed as he hurried along the path.

"The elephants are just through here," he said. "They're a really lovely group. Saran, the matriarch, is in her fifties. She's really smart and keeps everyone in line."

"How's the health of the herd?" Max asked. "Any signs of arthritis in the older animals?"

Zoe knew that elephants could sometimes suffer from pain and inflammation in their leg joints – hardly a surprise when they could weigh up to 2700 kilograms – and could even become overweight if they didn't have enough room to exercise.

"Not so far," Joe replied. "No foot rot or nail cracks or other issues, either – we've trained them to lie down so we can check their feet are healthy. In fact, they're all in good shape, from head to toe."

He seems proud of that, Zoe thought. Pawprints Zoo might be a little neglected but it sounded as though the keeper really cared about his animals.

"That's good news," Max said, looking pleased. "Health problems would make the journey to their new home more stressful – for them and for you, Joe."

They rounded a bend in the path and Zoe saw a vast barn behind some hefty metal gates. On the left of that, there was a large sandy enclosure, where an elephant almost twice as tall as Zoe was watching them from the other side of a stone-walled ditch. It stared at them, long trunk trailing all the way to the ground. Two beautiful cream-coloured tusks gleamed in the autumn sunlight and its wide ears flapped back and forth as they got nearer, making Zoe wonder if it was saying hello. She knew elephants used their ears as well as their trunks to communicate.

"This is Babu," Joe said, pausing beside the stretch

of wall in front of the elephant. "He's the bull of the herd. We find he quite often keeps himself to himself, for at least part of every day, because that's how it would be in the wild. Ade, our other male, is his son but he's still young and spends most of his time with the cows."

Zoe blinked in confusion. *Cows?* Then she remembered that female elephants were called cows, just like male elephants were bulls and young ones were calves. They watched as Babu dipped his trunk into a water trough and sprayed water high into the air over his back. Joe smiled. "He's got a cheeky sense of humour. I've lost count of the number of times he's caught me out and given me a soaking."

Zoe smiled as she studied Babu across the walled ditch. Was it her imagination or were his eyes twinkling? "I like him."

"He's got quite a personality," Joe said. "They all do, even Dodie. She might only be four months old but she's a character already."

Zoe felt a fizz of anticipation as Oliver peered around. "Where is she?"

"She's with her mum and the other elephants," Joe explained. "They're in the big building over to the right."

"Can we see her?" Oliver asked.

"Not so fast," Max said. "We're here to find out more about the whole herd, not just fuss over the baby. There'll be plenty of time to meet Dodie later."

Oliver looked as disappointed as Zoe felt – they were both desperate to meet the youngest member of the herd. But he did his best to hide it. "Yeah, you're right. Sorry, Dad."

Max clapped a hand onto his son's shoulder. "Why don't you two have a look around? Come back here in twenty minutes or so and you can meet all the other elephants. That's okay, isn't it, Joe?"

The elephant keeper nodded. "It should be fine. Just keep away from the bits that are taped off."

Zoe exchanged a look with Oliver; between the taped-off areas and the empty enclosures it didn't feel as though there was much to see at Pawprints. But it was clear her dad and Max had business to discuss with Joe and so she shrugged. "Okay. See you in a while."

The adults headed towards the gates. Zoe heard the jangle of keys and turned to Oliver. "Want to play spot the animals? Babu doesn't count."

Oliver let out a grumpy huff. "It'll be a short game."

"Come on," Zoe said, setting off back the way they'd come. "There must be something else here."

But as they suspected, the animals were few and far between. Eventually, Zoe found some rabbits near the petting zoo, who were clean and comfortable and didn't seem to mind the quietness around them. To Zoe, the empty enclosures and eerie silence felt all wrong – every zoo she'd ever been to had been busy.

Oliver was subdued too. "I wonder if this is how Tanglewood might have ended up," he said as they walked. "If your parents hadn't bought it, I mean."

Zoe almost shuddered. Tanglewood had needed

some attention when the Fox family had first arrived but it hadn't been as run-down as Pawprints.

"But they did buy it," she said, dredging up a smile. "And look – here's the reptile house. I bet there's something in here."

A wall of moist heat hit them the moment they pushed open the door. Zoe's guess had been right – there was a long, thick green anaconda coiled up half-in and half-out of the water behind a thick floor-to-ceiling pane of glass, and a vivarium containing several giant land snails.

"It says there's a bird-eating spider in here," Zoe exclaimed, bending down to peer into a dusty tank set into the wall. It was filled with mottled brown bark and dark-green leaves but she thought she could just about make a shadowy shape. "And there it is – I can see it!"

Oliver didn't even glance across – he kept his gaze fixed on the anaconda. "Cool."

"Come and see," Zoe insisted. "It's huge, almost as big as my hand."

He ambled over and looked briefly into the tank. "Oh, yeah. Great."

"If you look closely, you can see all the hairs on its legs – it uses those to sense movement and catch its prey." She sharpened her gaze. "Oh, I think we woke it up!"

Oliver straightened up. "Maybe we should be heading back."

"Okay," Zoe said slowly, trying not to stare at him. "You're probably right."

She was deep in thought as they left the humid heat of the reptile house. This was the first time she'd ever seen Oliver less than fascinated by an animal or creature. And now that she came to think about it, she wasn't sure she'd ever seen him visit Tanglewood's Moonbeam Mansion, where the creepy-crawlies lived alongside the park's nocturnal residents. Zoe would be the first to admit that she'd never been a fan of bugs but the more time she spent watching them, the more interested she'd become. And spiders like tarantulas were so big that she thought of them more as animals, anyway. Oliver clearly didn't share her fascination.

Shaking her head in puzzlement, she glanced across at him – Tanglewood was hosting a Meet the Monsters event during the half-term holiday, designed to show people that the creatures they often feared, like snakes, bats and spiders, weren't really scary at all. Maybe that would capture Oliver's interest...

Some of the Pawprints signposts had fallen down, which made finding the way back to the elephant house tricky, but they got there after a few wrong turns. There was no sign of Babu now, or the adults, so Zoe and Oliver followed the path that led around the side of the sandy enclosure. And as they passed some overgrown branches, Zoe saw a sight that filled her with delight – Dodie the baby elephant!

She was standing between two much larger elephants, although they weren't as big as Babu. Even so, their bulk made Dodie seem even smaller. Zoe shook away a smile – compared to most other babies she was still enormous! Her grey skin was covered with patches of fuzzy hair and unlike the adults, she had no tusks on either side of her trunk. In fact, her trunk seemed to be giving her some trouble – the others had no problem lifting their much longer trunks high into the air to curl back and touch their foreheads, but Dodie's wobbled and twisted around as if it was on an invisible string. One of the adults reached down with her own trunk and seemed to stroke Dodie's head, ears flapping as though she was reassuring the infant she wasn't alone.

"Which one is the matriarch?" Oliver whispered, glancing back and forth between the elephants.

"No idea," Zoe admitted. "Maybe the biggest?"

As they watched, Dodie turned to the nearest elephant and reached up to burrow her mouth into the older animal's belly. Oliver grinned. "That must be Dodie's mum. Baby elephants drink milk from their mother when they're small and don't eat solid food for months after they're born."

"Like humans," Zoe agreed.

"And look," Oliver said, pointing to the doorway of the elephant house. "That must be the juvenile."

Zoe tore her gaze away from Dodie to follow Oliver's outstretched finger. "Oh!" She let out a tiny squeal as she saw a young bull elephant about twice as big as Dodie heading towards his family. His tusks were much smaller than those of the adults, but she could tell he would be huge when he was fully grown. "I think you're right. What's his name again – is it Alfie?"

"I think Dad said it was Ade," Oliver said.

"Ade," Zoe repeated, getting a warm feeling as she watched the other elephants raise their trunks to greet the young bull. "So that's Babu and Dodie and Ade we know so far."

A flash of movement caught the edge of Zoe's vision. A moment later, Max and Zoe's dad appeared from further along the path with Joe.

"Hello," Max said, smiling. "Have you had fun exploring?"

Zoe hesitated; Pawprints was so run-down that she wouldn't use the word fun exactly…but what else could they say? She nodded politely. "Yes, thanks. We found the reptile house."

Joe looked pleased. "That's good news. It's one of the few exhibits we have left. The anaconda is going to Edinburgh Zoo early next week."

"What about the bird-eating tarantula?" Zoe asked.

"Destined for Madrid," Joe said. "Pretty soon everything will be gone."

There was a note of sadness in his voice and Zoe thought she knew why. "You're going to miss the elephants."

"That shouldn't be a problem, actually," Dad said. "Elephants bond very strongly with their keepers and it takes a long time to build up trust and a relationship. Luckily, Joe has agreed to move with them."

Zoe felt her eyes widen as she worked out what her dad was saying. "So you mean—"

"It's official?" Oliver cut in, looking every bit as excited as Zoe felt. "Babu and Dodie and the others are moving to Tanglewood?"

Joe nodded. "Yes, that's right. We're all coming. On Tuesday, in fact, providing Babu decides to cooperate. He – uh – doesn't like travelling much."

Zoe pictured the enormous bull elephant. "I bet he doesn't. You must need a giant truck to fit him into."

"We've got two specially reinforced lorries coming all the way from Chester Zoo," Max explained. "One for Babu and one for the rest of the herd."

"Won't he mind travelling on his own?" Zoe asked, thinking about how upset Tindu the tiger had been by his journey to Tanglewood. It had taken him a while to settle in afterwards, although he was very happy now.

"He's probably the only one who won't mind," Joe said. "The others are very close – splitting them up, even for a little while, could be upsetting, especially for Dodie and Ade."

"And that's the last thing we want," Zoe's dad said. "But I'm sure the matriarch will calm the others down. That's one of her jobs within the herd."

Joe pointed over to the elephant in the corner. "That's her there – she's called Saran. Sometimes you can tell which elephant is the oldest by the folds in their ears, but the most reliable way is by looking at their teeth. Did you know they get through six sets of teeth in their lives?"

Six? Zoe thought faintly, remembering how grumpy Rory had been when he'd been teething a few years earlier. *Imagine going through that six times...*

Beside her, Oliver nodded. "It's because of their diet. They're herbivores so they only eat vegetation, but that includes things like tree bark and grasses, which they grind up into tiny pieces."

"Oh, so their teeth wear out?" Zoe guessed. "And then they need to grow a new set to replace them."

Joe looked impressed. "You guys know your

elephant facts. I can see we're going to feel very at home at Tanglewood."

Zoe shared an excited look with Oliver. "I think you're going to fit right in," she said, smiling.

Chapter Three

Zoe found it hard to think about anything except the elephants for the rest of weekend. Mum was working hard with Tanglewood's builders and gardening teams to make sure everything was ready when Saran and the herd arrived, and Zoe could almost taste the excitement. It was nearly thrilling enough to make her forget about her upcoming birthday, until she dreamed all the elephants came to her party, dressed in pink ballet tutus... By Sunday afternoon, Zoe had decided she needed a break from non-stop elephants and headed into the park to see if any of the keepers needed her help.

She stopped by the tiger house first. There was a small crowd outside, gazing into the enclosure, and Zoe soon saw why: Tindu was snoozing in a patch of autumn sunlight, his orange-and-black fur glowing like flames. Zoe wasn't surprised to find him asleep – in the wild, a big cat might sleep for eighteen to twenty hours every day. And snoozing was actually a good thing for Tindu – it showed how comfortable and relaxed the tiger had become in his new habitat. Tanglewood's other tiger, Koko, didn't seem to sleep as much – she liked to prowl around or play with the giant boomer balls that the keepers had scattered around the enclosure. Zoe saw a flash of orange among the leaves on the other side of the tigers' pen; that would be Koko, patrolling her territory.

Zoe spent a few moments watching both tigers, smiling when Tindu's paws began to twitch – was he dreaming about stalking through the wilds of

Sumatra, in search of his dinner? Eventually, Zoe dragged herself away – she could spend all day watching the tigers but that was the trouble with Tanglewood; getting too caught up with one animal meant she was sure to be missing out on something else. More visitors were gathered around the red-panda enclosure, gazing over the unfenced low wall with interest. As Zoe got nearer, she saw Abie the keeper inside. She was in the middle of a keeper talk. Zoe stopped to listen.

"We have two red pandas here at Tanglewood," Abie was saying. "Hardeep is a young male, he's four years old and you can see him now in his favourite spot, curled up amongst the highest branches of the tree."

The crowd looked up and gasped as they spotted the small, rusty-red creature draped along one of the branches. Zoe grinned; it looked a bit like a raccoon. She wondered how many of the visitors had been expecting to see a more colourful version of the famous black-and-white pandas?

"People are often surprised by the size of the red panda," Abie went on, "especially compared to the giant panda. As you can see, they look very different and you might be surprised to hear that they're not actually related to each other, although they both love to eat bamboo. Giant pandas are mostly found in China while red pandas tend to hang out in the Eastern Himalayan mountains, although there are some parts of China where you'd find both species."

There was a rustling sound as a black, whiskery nose appeared among the bamboo foliage behind Abie's head, followed by a curious cat-like face with two pointy white ears. The creature bustled along a log towards Abie, its bushy tail waving in the air. The crowd *aah*ed, making Zoe smile – up close, red pandas were incredibly cute.

"These guys spend a lot of their time in trees and, as you can see, Hardeep is very happy up there." Abie turned her attention to the other red panda, who had stopped beside her at head height and was waiting expectantly. "But Kushpu here doesn't usually climb as high as Hardeep and that's partly because she was born with a club foot. If you look closely, you'll see that her back leg is deformed, which means she can't grip the branches as tightly when she climbs."

Instead of a foot that ended in claws, Kushpu's back left leg was more of a solid stump. It didn't seem to bother the little creature, as far as Zoe could tell, but she knew that Abie had to give her special exercises to make sure the muscles were stretched in the right way. Like many of the animals at Tanglewood, the red pandas took part in training with their keeper, which helped to keep them entertained but also helped to ensure they stayed healthy.

Abie picked up a thin stick with a yellow ball on the end and held it just over Kushpu's head. Instantly, the red panda reared up onto her back paws and stretched up to high-five the ball.

"As you can see, Kushpu copes really well with her disability," Abie told the chuckling crowd, offering the red panda a berry as a reward. "We use training like this to teach our animals lots of different responses, so that they trust us and know what to do when the vet comes to check their paws or their tummies."

Zoe watched as Abie encouraged Kushpu to turn around and touch the ball, feeding her a treat each time she did so. The air was filled with quiet clicks as people snapped photos. After a short while, Abie lowered the stick and smiled at her audience. "I hope you've enjoyed the talk. Let me know if you have any questions."

The crowd clapped and began to drift away. Abie caught sight of Zoe and waved. "Perfect timing, Zoe, I'm just about to give Kushpu a proper workout. Want to give me a hand?"

Zoe nodded hard. There was nothing she liked better than getting close to Tanglewood's animals and she'd never actually seen Kushpu's special exercise routine. Hurrying forward, she waited for Abie to open the double-locked gate and let her inside the enclosure.

Once the gate was safely locked again, Abie held out the training stick for Kushpu to touch. "I'll just get her attention again and then we'll move to the back of the enclosure, where it's a bit quieter."

She fed the red panda a morsel of fruit as a reward and then pointed along the log. Kushpu walked along it and jumped to a small platform that was shaded from public view by some bamboo.

"Now the hard work begins, Kushpu," Abie said with a smile. She lifted a camera from around her neck and handed it to Zoe. "We need some photos for our social-media accounts. Do you think you could snap a few pictures?"

"Of course!" Zoe said, thrilled to be asked.

She was always taking photographs of the animals on her phone but it was a big responsibility to use one of Tanglewood's expensive cameras. Abie hung the camera around Zoe's neck and showed her which buttons to press.

"If you hold this button down, it will take several

pictures at once," the keeper explained. "Then we can choose the best ones."

Zoe lifted the camera and peered at the screen to make sure Kushpu was in the shot.

"Okay," she said, her finger poised over the button on the top. "I'm ready."

Abie began to put the red panda through her paces. She started with some simple stretches similar to the ones Zoe had seen her do during the keeper talk. Then Abie held the training stick further up, encouraging Kushpu to stretch higher and reach both paws over her head to touch the yellow ball. The camera clicked furiously as Zoe snapped photo after photo.

"She looks like a ballerina," she said, grinning as Kushpu lifted her club foot and balanced for a moment on her good leg, clasping both front paws on the ball above her.

"It's funny you should say that," Abie replied, rewarding the red panda with a chunk of juicy-looking pear. "Kushpu's exercises are actually inspired by ballet poses – they give her muscles a really good stretch and help her to stay strong."

As she spoke, she switched the training stick to her left hand and held it out behind Kushpu. "Backwards," she commanded and the panda obediently stretched her deformed leg out to tap the ball.

Zoe laughed. "We should put on a panda production of *The Nutcracker* for Christmas. Everyone would love it."

"I'm not sure Hardeep would enjoy it," Abie said with a smile, glancing up at the other red panda snoozing among the high branches. "He's not as elegant as Kushpu."

The keeper continued to work with Kushpu, encouraging her to stretch her leg with every task while Zoe took more photos. Eventually, Abie pulled out a large piece of pear and gave it to the red panda.

"Good workout today, Kushpu," she said, as the little creature bustled away with her reward.

"I got some great pictures," Zoe said, handing the

camera back to Abie. "I'm sure it looked like Kushpu was smiling in some of them."

Abie grinned. "I do think she enjoys it. And she loves the camera too. Hardeep is a bit shy but Kushpu loves the limelight." She took the camera. "Thanks for helping me out. I'll let you know when the pictures go online."

"No problem," Zoe replied. "Kushpu is really cute. Maybe I could take some more photos next time you're training her?"

"Of course! And I'll be sure to tell the other keepers you can handle a camera." Abie unlocked the gate and stepped outside. "You can be our unofficial Tanglewood photographer."

A warm rush of pride flowed through Zoe. "I'd like that."

Abie nodded. "Let me know if you need to borrow the camera. Thanks again, Zoe."

She waved and disappeared along one of the paths. Zoe hurried back towards Tanglewood Manor, her mind racing with ideas for photographs she might take around the park. There was certainly no shortage of magnificent animals to take pictures of, although she wasn't sure she'd find anything cuter than Kushpu in her ballet poses. But with Dodie and the other elephants arriving on Tuesday and the Savannah Safari due to open in less than two weeks, there'd be even more to capture through the lens of a camera. Zoe couldn't wait to get started!

Chapter Four

Zoe did not want to go to school on Tuesday.

"My tooth hurts," she complained at breakfast, holding the side of her face.

Mum raised her eyebrows. "I don't suppose that has anything to do with the arrival of six elephants later today, has it?"

Zoe felt her cheeks grow warm. "Maybe." She probed her tooth with her tongue. "But I do have toothache."

"Wrap up warm today and we'll see how it is later," Mum said, handing her a thick woolly scarf. "Now, off you go or you'll miss the bus."

Oliver was waiting at the bus stop outside the Tanglewood gates and he looked just as dejected as Zoe felt.

"I can't believe we're missing all the excitement again," he complained. "It's just like when Tindu and Koko arrived – stupid school gets in the way of everything!"

Zoe nodded. "It does. Although we'd probably have to keep out of sight when the elephants actually arrived. They'll need time to settle in, just like Tindu."

"But it will be easier for the elephants," Oliver replied, frowning. "There's a whole group of them and they'll all be moving together. I just wish we could be here."

It felt to Zoe as though the day went on for ever, but at last the final bell rang and she was free. She and Oliver tumbled off the bus and went their separate ways to change out of their school uniforms. No one was at the manor house when Zoe arrived – the kitchen was empty; no Mum and no Rory. Instead, there was a note on the table: *Come to the elephant house!* After swapping her school uniform for her Tanglewood clothes, Zoe tugged on her wellies and set off as fast as she could.

The building where the elephants would sleep was at the edge of a large, sandy-floored paddock that led into the vast grassy fields of the Savannah Safari. Like all the new enclosures at Tanglewood, it was eco-friendly, with a rainwater collection system to recycle rainfall and solar panels in the roof to help keep the energy costs down. Zoe's mum had also tried to keep the fencing as light as possible, so that visitors could stand and watch the elephants – that meant there was a waist-high wall with a deep ditch on the other side between the public path and the sandy paddock, but no tall walls, wire or windows.

Mum was waiting next to the wall with Rory.

"There you are," she said, as Zoe jogged towards them. "How was school? How's your tooth?"

Zoe craned her head to see into the paddock, which was disappointingly empty.

"Hmmm?" she said in a distracted voice. "Oh, it's all fine. My toothache has gone."

"The elephants are inside," Rory told her helpfully. "One of them did a poo. Did you know that they poo between fifteen and twenty times a day?"

Zoe tried not to laugh. "Wow, I didn't know that. What else do you know about elephants?"

Her little brother's face creased up as he thought. "Their trunks are so strong they can push down trees and they use them to pick up small things like twigs and stones too." He waved his arm in front of his face. "Like this!"

He was just about to pick up a pebble from the ground when Oliver skidded to a halt behind them, out of breath from running. "Did I miss anything?"

Rory straightened up. "One of the elephants did a p—"

"Enough about that, Rory," Mum interrupted, sounding exasperated. "I think we all know animals poo by now."

Oliver flashed a grin at Zoe. Mucking out was part of everyday life when you lived in a zoo.

"Our new arrivals had a good journey," Mrs Fox went on. "They're inside with Joe and Max, getting a health check, and then they should be coming outside for a little while to have a look around their new home."

Zoe hugged herself with breathless anticipation. She hoped Oliver was right and that the elephants settled in fast at Tanglewood. Surely it would help that they had their keeper, Joe, with them? And Saran would help to calm the rest of the herd down.

"Did you know that elephants use rumbles as a way to reassure the others that everything is okay?" she asked Oliver. "It sounds a bit like they're purring, or as though their stomach is rumbling."

He nodded. "And they use their trunks to trumpet when there's danger. If they see a threat in the wild, the adult elephants make a circle and put all the calves in the middle to keep them safe."

Zoe nodded. Healthy adult elephants didn't need to worry about predators like lions or hyenas, but baby elephants were different – they could easily become a meal and needed the protection of the herd. The only danger a fully grown elephant couldn't handle was a human with a gun – a poacher who wanted their precious tusks to sell as part of the illegal ivory trade – but Zoe didn't want to mention that in front of her little brother.

"Look," she said, pointing at the elephant house. "The door is opening!"

Mum and Rory turned around and Zoe held her breath as her dad appeared in the doorway. He held up one hand in a thumbs-up gesture and then pushed one of the oversized double doors all the way back. Max did the same on the other side. A moment later, Zoe saw Joe. And then she saw the edge of a tusk. A moment later, the doorway was filled by an elephant with its trunk curled up high and back so that it touched the top of the animal's head. Its mouth was open as though it was smiling and it glanced carefully left and right, taking everything in.

Zoe clenched her fists with excitement, half-hoping they'd be treated to a triumphant trumpet, but that would mean that the elephants sensed danger. They were probably communicating in other ways, using sounds that were too low for human ears to pick up. Zoe glanced over at Oliver, who looked every bit as enthralled as she felt.

"Is that Babu?" he asked in an awestruck voice.

Mrs Fox shook her head. "No, that's Saran. Elephants take their lead from the matriarch. Bulls can be a tiny bit temperamental sometimes, so I expect Babu will be let out separately, to make sure he doesn't get spooked by his new surroundings. A stampeding bull elephant is incredibly dangerous."

Apparently deciding the new environment was safe, Saran flapped her enormous ears and lumbered into the enclosure. Seconds later, another adult elephant appeared in the doorway, following Saran.

This one was holding its trunk up and back too, exactly the way the matriarch had. *It must mean something*, Zoe decided as she watched the stately procession, making a mental note to ask Joe about it. And then the thought flew out of her head as the calf, Ade, appeared. He looked small compared to the other two elephants, until little Dodie tottered into view. She did not have her trunk balanced on top of her head – she was trying to hold on to Ade's tail, but it was obvious she didn't have much control over the muscles in her trunk and so she kept losing her grip.

"Aw!" Zoe couldn't help exclaiming.

"She is very cute," Mum said, smiling.

Right behind Dodie was the final female elephant, bringing up the rear of the herd and protecting the younger ones from predators, exactly the way she would in the wild.

Oliver counted them quickly. "Five. Babu must still be inside."

"Is that Dodie's mother?" Zoe asked, pointing to the elephant at the back.

"Yes, I think that's Tembo," Mrs Fox said. "She's Ade's mum too – he is Dodie's older brother. Babu is their dad."

"That means the elephant who came out second must be the auntie," Oliver said. "Although I don't think she's actually Saran's daughter."

"That's right," Mrs Fox said. "Raja isn't directly related to any of the animals she lives with but that doesn't really mean anything. Elephants form close-knit herds and all the adult cows help to look after the young ones, the way an auntie might in a human family."

Now that all the elephants were outside, Joe approached Saran. He called out a greeting first, making sure she knew he was there, and then moved nearer. Zoe noticed that her dad and Max kept out of the way. *They know the elephants don't trust them yet*, she thought. Joe reached into a bucket and pulled something out.

"Apple quarters," Mum explained. "See how the others are waiting for Saran to eat first?"

It was true; Saran's trunk had snaked forwards to take the apple from Joe's outstretched hand and the others were simply standing back and watching, showing no signs of coming forward to get their share. Even Ade stayed where he was. Zoe couldn't imagine the same thing happening with the guinea pigs or the meerkats – it was every creature for themselves when the treats came out.

"They know who the boss is," Mum went on. "Elephants are big on good manners – the older a female is, the more respect she gets from the herd. I suppose you could say she's a bit like a queen – except that no one else can eat until she's finished!"

Zoe watched as Saran took the chunks of apple with her trunk and tipped them into her mouth. "She uses it just like a hand."

"A hand with no bones," Oliver said. "Just loads of muscles."

Mum nodded. "If you look closely, you'll see African elephants have two little fingers on the end of their trunks, which help them to pick up very small things without too much trouble."

Saran isn't having any trouble with those apple pieces, Zoe thought with a grin. After a few more minutes, the older elephant lowered her trunk and took a step backwards. That seemed to be some kind of signal to the others because a sea of trunks suddenly floated towards Joe.

"One at a time," he called, laughing. "I can't keep up!"

He split the remaining treats between Ade, Tembo and Raja. Dodie was too young for solid food – she got all her nutrition from her mother's milk – and Zoe saw she was looking round her new home with bright, inquisitive eyes. Something must have caught her attention because she started to move away, but Raja's long trunk curled around her before she'd taken more than a few steps and nudged her gently back into the herd.

"See what I mean?" Mum said, smiling. "Everyone looks after the baby."

Once the apples were finished, Joe stepped back.

"Off you go," he said to the elephants. "Have a look around before it gets too dark."

It was almost as though Saran understood him because she lifted her head and took a good look around. Then she raised her head and flapped her ears, letting out a long, low rumble. She lifted one foot for a moment and waited, almost as though she was making sure everyone was paying attention, before lumbering off towards the grassy area of the paddock. Tembo and Raja followed, ushering Ade and Dodie in front of them. Joe, Max and Mr Fox grouped together in the empty paddock for a huddled conversation and Zoe wondered if they were discussing when to release Babu.

Mum glanced at Oliver and Zoe. "So, what do you think? Are Tanglewood's visitors going to like our latest additions?"

"Are you kidding?" Oliver burst out. "They're going to love them!"

Zoe nodded enthusiastically. "Yes, they're fantastic."

"No," Rory said, his small face solemn. "They're not fantastic."

Zoe gaped at him – she'd never known her little brother to dislike an animal before. "What—?"

Rory's face split into an enormous grin. "They're elephantastic!"

Everyone laughed.

"You're right, Rory," Mum said, ruffling the little boy's hair fondly. "We might have to put that on our new posters!"

Chapter Five

Zoe awoke in the night with a sharp pain in her jaw. She lay there for a few moments, listening to the wind and the rain outside, testing each of her teeth until she found the problem. It was the same tooth that had hurt the day before, the one she'd mentioned to her mum; the pain had gone away not long after that and she'd forgotten all about it. But now it was back, much worse than before.

Closing her eyes, Zoe tried to get back to sleep,

but the nagging ache kept her awake. With a sigh, she pushed back her covers and padded along the hallway to her parents' bedroom.

"Mum, wake up," she whispered, once she'd picked her way towards the bed. "I've got toothache."

Mum shifted sleepily and reached out to put on the bedside lamp. "Again? How bad is it?"

"I can't sleep."

With a bleary-eyed glance at the clock, Mum swung her legs out of bed. "Okay. Let's get you some medicine."

After giving Zoe two mouthfuls of the same sticky liquid Rory had when he was ill, Mum herded Zoe back to bed. "It should start to work soon. Try to get back to sleep."

Zoe nodded and said goodnight. She lay there in the darkness, trying to ignore the throbbing in her cheek, wondering what the elephants were doing now. They'd be safely tucked up inside their centrally heated house, of course, with plenty of warm straw to lie down on and snacks in case they got hungry in the night; elephants needed a lot of food to keep them going. Were Dodie and Ade lying awake like Zoe, listening to the rain rattling against the roof? Or were they fast asleep like Rory? She hoped they weren't too troubled by their new home – Joe had seemed very pleased with the way they'd settled in so far and he knew them best. *Maybe there's nothing to worry about*, Zoe thought with a yawn, as the medicine soothed her aching tooth. She let her eyes drift shut and fell asleep thinking of the elephants.

"Abie was looking for you," Mum said on Wednesday afternoon, as Zoe hunted through the kitchen cupboards for an after-school snack. "She said she'd be at the red-panda enclosure until closing time if you're heading into the park."

Zoe tore open the wrapper of a cereal bar and bit into it, taking care to chew on the side of her mouth that didn't hurt. "Okay, I'll go and find her once I've got changed," she said in between mouthfuls.

"I wonder what she wants."

"I expect she wants you to take more photos," Mum said. "The last ones were very good."

Zoe beamed with pleasure. "Thank you. But Kushpu is so cute that she made it easy to take her picture." She aimed a questioning glance at her mother. "Do you think I'll be able to take photos of the other animals? Abie said I could borrow a camera – maybe if I get some good shots of the elephants, you could use them on the posters."

Mum thought for a moment. "Okay, let me talk to Dad, we'll see what we can do. I can't promise anything."

"Thanks, Mum," Zoe said. She took a large bite of her snack and winced. "Ow!"

"Is that tooth still hurting?" Mum asked, looking concerned. "I think I'd better ring the dentist."

Zoe rubbed at her cheek – her toothache didn't seem to be getting any better. "I suppose so," she mumbled, throwing what was left of the cereal bar in the bin.

Mum picked up her phone and tapped at the screen. After a short conversation, she hung up. "We've got an appointment tomorrow after school."

Zoe threw her a dismayed look. "But I told Oliver I'd help him to groom the zebras."

"I'm sure he can manage without you," Mum said in a firm voice. "No arguments, Zoe. You need to get that tooth looked at – you don't want to be miserable with toothache on your birthday, do you?"

"I suppose not," Zoe said, picturing an enormous cake that she couldn't eat. "Okay, I'll let Oliver know I can't help him."

Mum looked satisfied. "Good. Now, hadn't you better go and get changed? You don't want to keep Abie waiting."

The sun was just starting to cast long shadows over the park as Zoe hurried towards the red panda's home. The paths felt chilly and dark and made Zoe wrap her fleece more tightly around herself. *It'll soon be winter*, she thought as she passed Snowy Point, shivering slightly at the thought. It was all right for the snow leopards – Minty and Tara had thick, furry coats to keep them warm. How would Dodie and the other elephants cope, with no fur to keep out the cold? It was a good job their new enclosure was fitted with a heated pool – maybe they'd spend the whole winter in the warm water.

Abie was leaning against the wall of the red-panda enclosure, watching Kushpu chewing on some bamboo.

"Hi, Zoe," she called. "Did your mum tell you I was looking for you?"

Zoe nodded. "Yes. It is about the photos?"

"That's right," Abie said, smiling. "The ones you took on Sunday were great. They've gone down really well on our social-media accounts. But the picture I really want to talk about is this."

She pulled out her phone and held it towards Zoe. The picture on the screen made Zoe laugh out loud. It was a photo of Kushpu balancing on one leg, her furry red forelegs high over her head as she grasped the training ball.

"She looks like a prima ballerina," Zoe said, giggling. "All she needs is a tutu."

Abie laughed. "Exactly. And look, that photo has had over five thousand likes. It's gone viral!"

Zoe peered at the numbers underneath the photo: Abie was right; it had a huge number of likes.

"Wow," she breathed in amazement.

"We've had a big spike in enquiries about our 'Meet the Red Pandas' experience. And I hear ticket sales for this weekend have shot up," Abie went on. "We think that's down to you and Kushpu."

Zoe stared at her. "But – but it can't be. People must have heard about the elephants – they're coming to see them."

Abie shook her head. "No, we haven't announced their arrival yet and the Savannah Safari isn't due to open for another ten days, so it can't be that, either." She patted Zoe on the arm. "Credit where credit is due – you took a great photo that has really captured people's imaginations. Well done!"

Zoe felt her cheeks grow warm with pride.

"Thank you," she said, giving Abie her phone back. "I'm happy to help."

"Give me a shout if you need to borrow a camera," Abie went on. "I'm sure there's a spare."

"I will," Zoe said, beaming at her. "Mum is going to ask Dad if I can photograph the elephants too so I might need it soon."

It was Zoe's turn to clean out the guinea pigs but she couldn't resist stopping by the elephant house first. The distant sound of heavy machinery filled the air as she passed the closed-off entrance to the Savannah Safari, and she imagined diggers trundling across the ground, smoothing out the road that the buses would take. A herd of gazelles would be arriving next week, to fill the paddock opposite the elephant enclosure. The fields next to the giraffes would contain some black rhinos and Zoe knew her parents had made plans to bring in a herd of endangered Rothschild giraffes in the near future. Tanglewood seemed to be getting bigger every week!

Zoe was disappointed not to be able to see Dodie when she arrived at the elephant house. Babu was there, rubbing his enormous tusks against one of the thick wooden poles dotted around the sand. Every now and then, he let out a low growl that made Zoe's hair stand on end – he sounded more like a T-Rex than an elephant.

Joe appeared from the elephant house, pushing a wheelbarrow, and Zoe guessed he was going to clear up some of the droppings she could see. He waved when he spotted her and came over.

"Hi, Zoe," he said. "Have you come to check up on us?"

She smiled. "I was on my way to muck out the guinea pigs and decided to say hello."

Joe held up a pair of heavy rubber gloves. "I'm on mucking-out duty too. Although I imagine cleaning up after the guinea pigs is easier that shovelling elephant poo."

"Much easier," Zoe agreed, grinning. "I bet Dad is going to need to buy a bigger dung container now that we've got six elephants at Tanglewood."

"Not all of it goes onto the dung pile," Joe said. "Some of it goes to the medical centre to be tested. A lot of animal droppings contain something called metabolites, which we can use to work out how stressed the animals are. I'm hoping we'll see low levels in the elephant dung, meaning the move hasn't worried them too much."

Zoe glanced over at Babu, who was still grumbling as he raised a giant foot to kick at a battered cardboard box, which Zoe guessed had been filled with treats for an earlier enrichment activity. The box flew along the ground, now looking even more crumpled.

"He doesn't sound very happy," she said.

Joe smiled. "Don't worry about Babu. He's just making sure everyone knows he's here and marking his territory, in case there are other bull elephants around. He'll be fine in a day or two, as soon as he realizes he's king of the hill."

Zoe thought of Sinbad, Tanglewood's male lion,

and Tindu; they both liked to make their presence felt with earth-shattering roars. It was definitely a boy thing, Zoe decided as she listened to Babu rumble on, although she sometimes thought that Koko the female tiger's roar was even louder than Tindu's.

"Where are the other elephants?" she asked.

"Out exploring," Joe replied. "In the wild, they might cover huge distances in their search for food and water. Matriarchs have great memories and can remember all the best places to eat – Saran is probably leading the herd to check out the local food spots."

Zoe pictured the elephants roaming the large enclosure, then thought back to the moment they had first appeared the day before. "Do they always put their trunks on their heads when they walk?"

"No, that's something we taught them at Pawprints, for safety," Joe explained. "We trained them to raise their trunks when we move them around to make sure they're concentrating on what we say and do – think of it as a signal that they need to pay attention."

"That makes sense," Zoe said. She glanced around the empty paddock and sighed. "I wish I could see them. I can't wait for the Savannah Safari to start running."

Joe smiled. "It's great that the herd has so much room here. The enclosures at Pawprints were okay but the facilities at Tanglewood are a dream come true. I know they're going to be very happy."

"Good," Zoe said, feeling a burst of delight at the elephant keeper's praise. "We're all very happy they're here too."

She said goodbye to Joe and headed over to the guinea pigs, but not before she'd taken another look at her picture of Kushpu on Tanglewood's social-media pages – it had almost six thousand likes now! If her parents said yes to her request to take more photos of the elephants and other animals, maybe it was something she and Oliver could do during the half-term holiday.

Zoe grinned as she made her way through the fading light. Between her birthday and the elephants, there was certainly plenty to look forward to in the weeks to come.

Chapter Six

"Ah, yes, I can see what the problem is."

The dentist straightened up and looked at Zoe with a sympathetic smile. "I'm afraid you need a filling."

Zoe closed her mouth and stared at him in panic. "What does that mean?"

"It means you have a tiny hole in the enamel of your tooth. Every time you touch it, with food or perhaps with one of your other teeth, it aggravates the nerves underneath and hurts. All we need to do is fill the hole."

Mum reached out to squeeze Zoe's hand. "It's quite a straightforward thing and it will stop your toothache."

The dentist nodded. "I'll need to take some X-rays, just to make sure there's no damage to the roots, but we should be able to fix your tooth by the weekend. And we'll give you a temporary filling today, to stop it hurting."

Zoe was allowed to look at the X-rays when they were ready and she was fascinated to see her own jaw picked out in white against the black background.

"Here are your teeth," the dentist explained, pointing to two rows of white blobs. "And here are your roots, going much further into your jaw. Those are what stop your teeth from falling out – if you have a problem with them, you know about it."

Zoe peered at the X-rays. "What are those, right at the back?"

"They're your wisdom teeth," he explained. "They

move down when you're older, so you'll have more teeth to chew with."

"Like elephant teeth," Zoe said, widening her eyes. "They get more teeth as they get older too."

"Not quite," Mum said. "Humans only have two sets of teeth that come down from above. Elephant teeth move along in a line as they get worn out, a bit like the way shopping moves along the belt in a supermarket."

The dentist looked amazed. "I've never had a conversation about elephant teeth before."

Zoe grinned. "That's because you've never treated a zookeeper's daughter before."

When they'd finished studying the X-rays, the dentist mixed up a paste to put in the temporary filling. He warned Zoe not to eat on that side of her mouth for a few hours and gave Mum another appointment, for Saturday morning.

"Wouldn't it be easier if I could just grow another tooth instead of getting a filling?" Zoe said as they drove back home.

"Of course," Mum said. "But elephants can have a lot of teeth problems too, especially when they get older and their last set of teeth wears away. It's not a perfect system."

"Hmmm," Zoe said, leaning back into her seat. "I think I'll steer clear of eating bark and grasses."

Mum laughed. "I think that's a very good idea."

By Saturday afternoon, the hole in Zoe's tooth was fixed and her mouth was back to normal. The sunshine was warm for October – she didn't need to wear her Tanglewood fleece, especially after she'd helped Oliver to muck out the zebras to make up for missing out on their grooming on Thursday. And whether it was due to the autumn sun or Kushpu's sudden online stardom, the park did seem busier than usual. There were big crowds all around Tanglewood, especially at the red-panda enclosure.

Once they'd finished their work, Zoe and Oliver

made their way through the crowds towards the elephant house. Zoe's parents had given their permission for her to take more photos so she'd borrowed a camera from Abie; both Zoe and Oliver were keen to get some pictures of Dodie and the other elephants to raise awareness ahead of the Savannah Safari opening the following weekend.

"I hope we actually get to see Dodie," Zoe said as they walked. "The last few times I've come over, the herd has been out exploring the fields."

Oliver nodded in sympathy. "Me too. I can't wait until we break up for half-term – I'm planning to spend as much of the holiday as I can watching the elephants."

They passed Moonbeam Mansion, which had a big poster for the Meet the Monsters event on the outside wall.

"I'm looking forward to that too," Zoe said. "Dad has invited one of the bat experts from London Zoo to come and give a talk."

"Hmmm," Oliver said, kicking at a stone. "I'm

not sure I can make it, actually. I've got a lot of – um – homework to do."

Zoe stopped walking to stare at him. "*Homework?*"

Oliver hunched his shoulders. "Yeah. Haven't you?"

"Of course I have," Zoe replied, starting to move again. "We're in the same year, remember? But I'm not going to let it keep me away from an awesome evening like this."

Oliver shrugged. "It doesn't sound that awesome to me."

"You should still come and support it," Zoe argued. "Even if it's just for a little while."

"I suppose," he said, sounding unenthusiastic.

He changed the subject as they left the public part of the zoo, and started talking about the Savannah Safari, but Zoe couldn't get over how strangely he was acting. It was almost as though he didn't want to Meet the Monsters. She thought back to how he'd behaved in the reptile house at Pawprints – he hadn't been able to get away fast enough, especially once he'd seen the bird-eating spider. Was Oliver secretly afraid of creepy-crawlies?

"Look!" Oliver exclaimed, breaking into her thoughts. "The elephants are here. And they're in the water!"

It was true! Tembo and her children were knee deep in the heated pool. Saran was standing a little way off, pulling some hay from the branches of a tree and watching Dodie and Ade play with their mother. Zoe let out a delighted laugh and hurried forwards, lifting her camera as she went. She pulled the cover off and placed her finger on the button to snap a photo just as Ade filled his trunk with water and squirted it high over his head. It landed with a resounding splat on his back and some of it splashed onto Tembo. She responded by making a fountain of her own. Between them, Dodie dipped her trunk in and out of the water, trying to copy her mother and brother.

"Poor Dodie," Zoe said, unable to stop herself from smiling at the baby elephant's attempts to squirt water. "She reminds me of Rory when he tries to do something he can't quite manage."

She passed the camera to Oliver and let him take some pictures while she watched the elephants play. She'd grown used to the sounds they made now – the rumbles and grunts they made to communicate, along with some complicated-looking ear-flapping. And she had been amazed at how much they used their trunks too – Joe had explained that elephants had poor eyesight but excellent hearing and an incredible memory for smells. They used their trunks to identify who was approaching – whether human or elephant – and to say hello or to calm another frightened elephant. There was even a special way of touching trunks that a younger elephant might use to greet an older one – something that was a little like bowing. Elephant etiquette was even more complicated than human manners!

In the pool, Dodie seemed to stumble and fell over.

"Oh!" Zoe gasped, as the water splashed over the

calf's head. But a second later, Tembo was there, curling her trunk around Dodie's sturdy body and helping her back on her feet.

"Don't worry, elephants can swim," Oliver said, lowering the camera. "They can even use their trunks as a snorkel."

"But maybe not when they're only a few months old," Zoe said. "Luckily, there's always a grown-up around to lend a helping trunk."

The door of the elephant house opened and Joe came out carrying a bucket of fruit, which he spread around the enclosure. Once again, the elephants waited until Saran had eaten her fill before helping themselves. And now that the pool was empty, Saran seemed in the mood to play – she waded in and gave herself a shower. Then she buried her trunk deep in the water and seemed to rummage around.

"What is she doing?" Oliver asked, frowning as Saran dipped her trunk into the water again.

Zoe and Oliver watched as the old elephant

repeated her actions until she seemed to find what she was looking for. Satisfied, she stepped delicately from the water and crossed the paddock to Joe. She nudged him with her trunk.

Oliver looked mystified. "Seriously, what is she doing?"

Joe didn't seem confused at all. He smiled at Saran and put his hand underneath the elephant's trunk. Zoe leaned forwards. "She's giving him something. Look, she just dropped it into his hand."

"Thanks, Saran," Joe said loudly, giving her a tiny bow. "I'll add it to my collection."

Noticing Zoe and Oliver watching, he made his way over to them.

"What was that all about?" Oliver called, as soon as Joe was close enough to hear him.

"Saran was just thanking me for the snacks," Joe said, reaching into his pocket to pull out a small, perfectly round stone. "She likes to give me little presents every now and then – every single one is exactly the same size and shape. She spends quite a bit of time looking for them and throws away any she doesn't think is right."

Zoe felt suddenly warm inside. "I think that's the loveliest thing I've ever heard."

Joe smiled. "I'm sure she'll give you a present one day, Zoe, maybe even for your birthday if she gets to know you in time. It takes a while to gain their trust but it's true what they say – elephants never forget."

"I'd love a present from Saran," Zoe said, beaming back at him. "But I don't mind if she misses my birthday – I'm happy just to watch her."

Oliver was gazing at the elephants. "Is Tembo wearing a bracelet on her leg?"

"She is," Joe replied. "It's actually a pedometer, something to count how many steps she takes. Elephants walk for miles in the wild but there's no need for them to do that in captivity, where their food is much easier to come by. Captive elephants can be at risk of becoming overweight, so by putting a pedometer on Tembo, we're tracking how far the herd travels in a day. That way we can see how the new fields are working for them and decide how to distribute their food so that they get the most exercise."

"Wow," Oliver said, shaking his head. "Elephants are high-maintenance animals."

"They are," Joe agreed, laughing. "But they're worth it."

Zoe watched Dodie nudging at one of the tyres hanging from a tree, lurching backwards in alarm as it swung towards her. The baby elephant watched the tyre mistrustfully for a few seconds, waiting until it stopped swinging, and then stepped forwards to nudge it again.

"They're totally worth it," Zoe whispered, lifting the camera once more.

Chapter Seven

On Monday evening, Zoe was passing Moonbeam Mansion on her way to visit Flash the baby zebra when she heard someone call her name. She stopped and looked around; it was almost closing time and the sky was darkening. The path behind and ahead of her was empty. Frowning, Zoe peered into the gloom – had she imagined the voice?

She began to walk again.

"Zoe, wait!"

This time there was a person attached to the voice. It was Shannon, the keeper in charge of the bats and other nocturnal animals, and she was leaning around the door of Moonbeam Mansion, smiling at Zoe.

"Congratulations for that great picture you took of Kushpu," Shannon said. "Abie says it's had over ten thousand likes now, which is totally amazing."

Zoe felt herself blush. "Kushpu did all the hard work. All I did was press a button."

Shannon shook her head. "No, it was great work. Well done. But that isn't actually what I wanted to talk to you about. You know about our Meet the Monsters evening next week, right?"

"Of course," Zoe said with a smile. "I can't wait for it!"

"Good," Shannon said. "The thing is, ticket sales have been a bit low and I wondered if it's because people are often a little bit scared of bats and spiders. So I thought you might be able to work your magic with the camera to show the public they're not so scary. What do you think?"

Zoe thought of Oliver. "I suppose it is harder to fall in love with a tarantula. They do tend to freak people out."

Shannon sighed. "You either love them or you hate them, I guess. But bats can be cute, especially fruit bats, and they aren't the only night-loving creatures we have. Have you been inside Moonbeam Mansion?"

"No," Zoe admitted, feeling embarrassed. "The guinea pigs and the zebras keep me pretty busy."

"Not to mention Kushpu, right?" Shannon said, smiling. "I'd be happy to introduce you to our nocturnal animals right now if you've got time? Maybe as an early birthday present."

Zoe hesitated. She really wanted to see Flash before he settled down for the night. But she wanted to meet the bats too; Shannon was right, it would be a wonderful birthday treat.

She tipped her head. "Okay. I'd love to meet them – thank you."

It took Zoe's eyes a moment to adjust to the gloom inside Moonbeam Mansion. The double doors had an extra layer of see-through plastic curtains cut into wide strips, which she guessed must be there to stop the bats escaping. They led into a dimly lit wide hall.

"The bats are through there," Shannon said, pointing to another door, which was covered by a double layer of plastic strips. "I expect you can smell them."

Zoe sniffed; the air was moist and fruity. She nodded.

"Moonbeam Mansion is home to a few other nocturnal creatures," Shannon went on. "Our sugar gliders live in this hall, next door to the aye-ayes and the bushbabies."

She pointed at a row of shadowy glass-fronted enclosures. All were filled with sloping tree branches and plenty of leaves. Fascinated, Zoe peered through the glass of the nearest enclosure. How could an animal called a bushbaby be anything other than cute? "I've heard of the aye-aye," she said. "They're a type of lemur, aren't they?"

"That's right," Shannon said, lowering her voice to a whisper. "They come from Madagascar, just like all the other types of lemur. Bushbabies are native to the African mainland and they're amazing jumpers. If we're really lucky they might be about to wake up."

Zoe gazed into each enclosure, her eyes straining for any sign of movement. The aye-ayes and the bushbabies must be still asleep, she decided – there was nothing moving at all among the foliage. But it was a different story in the sugar-glider enclosure; the leaves were shaking, as though something was walking behind them. Then she saw the gleam of shiny black eyes and the flick of a thin bushy tail.

"There," she murmured to Shannon. "Is that one of them?"

Shannon nodded. "Sugar gliders originally come from the rainforests of Australia and Indonesia. They got their name for two reasons, firstly because they have a thin layer of skin that stretches from their wrists to their ankles and allows them to glide through the air between the trees. And secondly, because they love anything sweet."

Zoe watched the leaves rustle, desperate for a closer look.

"I've got some fruit here," Shannon said, holding up a covered bowl. "Shall I see if I can tempt one of the sugar gliders with a piece?"

Wide-eyed, Zoe nodded. "Oh, yes please."

Pulling a bunch of keys from her pocket, the bat keeper opened a door in the wall and slipped inside. Moments later, she appeared inside the sugar-glider enclosure. She placed some melon along one of the tree branches at the front. Then she stepped back and vanished from view.

Zoe kept her gaze trained on the melon as Shannon joined her at the window again, hardly daring to breathe. Seconds ticked by and nothing happened, but then the leaves began to move again and Zoe let out a little gasp of delight as a furry grey animal no bigger than her hand poked a whiskery pink nose into view. It reached for the fruit with delicate claws and started to nibble, its enormous round eyes darting around as it ate.

"That's Hamish, the male of our group," Shannon explained in a quiet voice. "Sugar gliders are very sociable and live in colonies in the wild, a bit like bats. A lot of people think they're rodents, but they're actually related to koalas and kangaroos."

"So they're marsupials?" Zoe said, lifting her camera to snap a photograph of the cute creature enjoying his snack. "Do they have pouches to carry their babies?"

"Hamish doesn't but the females do," Shannon replied. "The babies often cling onto their mother's back as they leap from tree to tree. They aren't endangered but, like most tree-dwelling animals, their habitat is under threat from deforestation."

He really is cute, Zoe thought, taking a few more pictures and checking the screen. If she could get a good enough photo to use online then she was sure ticket sales for Meet the Monsters would soar.

"How is he looking?" Shannon asked, nodding at the camera.

"A bit dark," Zoe replied. "The low light in here means that I probably need the flash, but I don't think Hamish would like it much."

"No," the keeper agreed. "We'll have to think of another way to get his best side. But for now, shall we meet the bats?"

"Yes please," Zoe said, tearing her attention away from Hamish.

"I should probably warn you that our fruit bats are free-flying," Shannon said, pausing in front of the plastic strip curtain. "Imagine a butterfly house but with much bigger creatures. They won't hit you though – they're far too clever for that."

The first thing Zoe noticed when she went through the second curtain was the high-pitched squeaking. The bat enclosure was open, exactly as Shannon had described, with no glass or wire fencing. A low wall ran in the shape of a giant horseshoe, with branches and poles on the other side. Several pieces of half-eaten fruit lay dotted around but Zoe didn't see any bats, until she thought to look up. And there, dangling upside down from the ceiling right above her head, was a cluster of around thirty winged animals.

"So *that's* where the squeaking is coming from," she said, grinning at Shannon.

The bat keeper nodded. "Yes, they can be a noisy bunch, especially if they get cross with each other. But the noise is just chatter – fruit bats actually have good eyesight so they don't use sound to find their way around, like other bat species."

Zoe gazed up at the furry bodies all nestled together against the ceiling. They were cute too, although some of them seemed quite grumpy. Every now and then, one would turn to its neighbour and squeak angrily, as though they had said something insulting or trod on a toe.

Back at ground level, Shannon unlocked a gate in the wall and started to lay out the mixture of apple, melon and banana from her bowl. "Fruit bats also have an excellent sense of smell. It won't be long before they're all awake and fly down to get their breakfast."

Sure enough, the squeaking and fidgeting among the bats increased almost as soon as Shannon had finished putting out the fruit.

"Watch," she murmured.

The first bat disengaged from the ceiling and swooped past Zoe to land beside a slice of apple. She heard a whisper of leathery wings as it passed her ear. Another bat flew down, then another, until the room was filled with the soft flap of wings and contented squeaks. Zoe stood very still, enjoying the gentle breeze the bats had created.

"They're just like birds," she breathed. "Not scary at all."

Shannon sighed. "If only more people felt like you."

"Maybe they just need to experience this," Zoe said, watching the bats eat.

"Exactly – that's why we're holding the Meet the

Monsters evening, to help people understand that there's no reason to be scared of animals like these."

Zoe's forehead creased as a thought occurred to her. "Does Oliver ever come to Moonbeam Mansion?"

Shannon tilted her head. "Sometimes. Why?"

"No reason," Zoe said. She bit her lip – should she tell the bat keeper her suspicion? "He doesn't seem very keen to come to Meet the Monsters and I can't help wondering why. So I thought he might be scared of the bats or something—"

"It's not the bats that will be putting him off," Shannon said. "It's the spiders. He's not their biggest fan."

Zoe nodded; it was exactly as she'd thought. "Do you think he might be less afraid if he got to know them a bit better?"

"Probably," Shannon replied, her expression serious. "But that's the kind of decision he needs to make for himself. You can't force him to come."

"No, of course not," Zoe said. "But maybe if you

asked him to help you with the bats and Charlotte the tarantula was in the same room for the event, it might help him to see she isn't so scary."

Shannon looked thoughtful. "I see what you're getting at. Okay, let me run it past Max. If he thinks it's a good idea then we'll do it."

"Great," Zoe said, smiling as another bat swooped past her nose to land on a thick slice of melon. She raised the camera and focused on framing the perfect picture. "It's a long shot but it might just work!"

"Off into the park again?"

Mum looked up from her tablet and frowned as Zoe headed for the kitchen door on Tuesday afternoon. "I feel like I hardly see you these days."

Zoe grabbed an apple from the fruit bowl and bit into it. "I'm hoping to see the gazelles," she mumbled around a mouthful, referring to the new herd that had arrived for the Savannah Safari that morning. "And I haven't seen Dodie since Sunday."

Mum sighed. "I suppose it is an exciting time in the park. As long as you're not neglecting your other animal duties? Or your homework?"

"Of course not, Mum," Zoe said, thinking guiltily of the history project she'd only half finished. "And soon it will be too dark after school to see properly. Oliver and I have decided we need to spend as much time as possible with the elephants while we still can."

"I want to see the elephants too," Rory piped up from his seat at the kitchen table. "Can I come?"

Zoe hesitated. It wasn't her turn to clean out the guinea pigs or help with the zebras. She could take Rory into the park with her...

"Okay," she said with a smile. "Get your boots on."

The weather had stayed warm, although there was a touch of late-afternoon chill in the air as Zoe and Rory made their way through Tanglewood. They waved at Cassie the big-cat keeper and nodded to Abie, who was coaxing Hardeep and Kushpu down from the trees for the night. Rory chattered about his day at school as he walked and Zoe half listened as she gazed into the enclosures they were passing. *We're lucky to have so many different animals at Tanglewood*, she thought, remembering the sad and lonely atmosphere at Pawprints. *It's a good thing the elephant enclosure was almost ready or who knows where Saran and Dodie and the others would have ended up.*

Suddenly, she heard the sound of running feet behind her. She spun round to see Oliver racing towards her.

"Dad kept me talking for ages," he puffed, slowing to a walk. "I thought the elephants would be in bed by the time he finished."

Zoe laughed. "Let me guess: homework, right?"

Oliver pulled a face. "Yeah. Oh, and he wants me to help out at the Meet the Monsters evening next week. Shannon needs a hand with the bats."

"Oh," Zoe said, keeping her expression blank. "That's good."

"I suppose so," Oliver said, scowling. "I'd rather be helping with the elephants, though. Do you think we'll ever be allowed to get close to them?"

Zoe had wondered that herself, although she understood how important it was for the elephants to trust the people around them. The enormous animals might seem calm and caring around Ade and Dodie but their size made them dangerous, especially if they felt threatened. "Maybe. But I don't mind watching them for now – they're so amazing."

Joe and Mr Fox were standing by the wall of the elephant enclosure, watching the elephants play. Ade and Dodie were over by the tyres, Tembo and Saran seemed to be gossiping nearby and Raja was using her trunk to snort clouds of dirt over her head and body.

"She's giving herself a dust bath," Zoe guessed, as Raja flapped her ears to spread the dirt around. "Maybe she's hot."

"Hello," Dad said, reaching down to lift Rory up

so that he had a better view. "I might have known we'd see you three this afternoon."

"How are the gazelles?" Zoe asked. "Did they arrive safely?"

Dad smiled. "They had a good journey and seem to be enjoying their new paddock. You might even be able to see them tomorrow, for your birthday."

Zoe stared at him. "Really?"

He nodded. "The Savannah Safari tour buses are all ready to go, although they don't officially start rolling until the weekend. But I think we can arrange a sneak preview if you'd like one?"

She beamed at him in excitement. "Can Oliver come too? And Mum and Rory?"

"Of course," Dad said, laughing. "The more the merrier. You should get to see Saran and the other elephants exploring their fields too."

Just at that moment, a shrill and indignant trumpeting split the air. Zoe's head whipped towards the elephants – had Ade hurt himself on the tyres? But it wasn't Ade who had made the sound, it was

Dodie. She must have got in the way of Raja's dust bath because she was covered in dirt and she looked every bit as surprised as everyone else at the sound she'd made. Shaking off the dust, she took a deep breath and blew again.

Joe laughed. "It sounds as though Dodie has worked out she can trumpet. It's a skill calves often master when they're four or five months old."

"She looks so astonished," Zoe said, giggling as she took a photo of Dodie almost going cross-eyed staring at her own trunk.

"There'll be no stopping her now," Joe said and sure enough, Dodie screwed up her face to trumpet again.

The other elephants came up to her, touching her with their trunks and making soft rumbling sounds.

"They're congratulating her," Oliver said. "Look how happy they are."

But not all the elephants had come up to Dodie. Ade had stomped off in the opposite direction and was batting the hanging tyres with his tusks. Zoe heard a discontented grumbling coming from him. She blinked. "Is Ade *jealous*?"

"Probably," Joe said. "As the baby of the herd, Dodie gets a lot of attention and Ade can sometimes be a bit sulky about it. That sound he's making is called a baroo rumble and it means 'Woe is me'."

Zoe felt her mouth drop open. "You know what the noises they make mean? In *words*?"

Joe nodded. "Some of them. Elephant communication is fairly advanced – they make a lot of different noises. Most of them are subsonic, which means we don't even hear them."

The humans weren't the only ones who had noticed Ade's unhappiness. Saran had crossed the enclosure and seemed to be giving him a stern talking to. Whatever she said did the trick, because Ade stopped rumbling and approached Dodie, touching her head with his trunk.

"Saran keeps everyone in line," Joe explained. "She's in charge of making sure everyone behaves in the right way."

The baby elephant raised her head and trumpeted into her big brother's face, making everyone laugh. *I don't think I'll ever get bored of watching the herd,* Zoe thought, focusing the camera as the elephants continued to fuss over the baby. *They're my new favourite animals.*

Chapter Eight

Zoe woke up early on Wednesday morning, her tummy squiggling with excitement. For a moment, she didn't know why – then she remembered: it was her birthday!

She lay still for a moment, thinking about the day ahead. She had school to get through first but after that Oliver was coming for tea. Would they be able to take the very first ride on the Savannah Safari? What other surprises were in store?

Mum, Dad and Rory were already up and waiting for her when she went downstairs.

"Happy twelfth birthday, Zoe!" Mum said, giving her a hug.

Dad handed her a stack of cards and a large, beautifully wrapped present. "There'll be more presents later but we thought you might like to open this one now."

Putting the cards to one side, Zoe tore at the leopard-print paper. Inside, was a large photograph album.

"We thought you could print off some of the pictures you've taken and start your very own portfolio," Mum said.

"Thank you," Zoe said, smiling. "It's a great idea."

Rory came forward to tug an envelope from the pile of cards. "Open this next. It's from me."

Smiling, Zoe put the photo album down and ripped open the envelope. The card inside had a drawing of an elephant being fed by someone with long brown hair.

"That's you," Rory explained. "I wrote your name in it too."

"Thanks, Rory, it's wonderful," Zoe said, lifting the front of the card. A folded piece of paper fluttered to the floor. Frowning, Zoe bent down to pick it up and gasped as she read what it said.

"*You are invited to feed the elephants, today at 3.30 p.m.*" She gaped at her parents, open-mouthed. "Really? I can *really* feed them?"

Mum laughed. "Yes! Joe says it will be fine, although it will probably just be Saran. Is that okay?"

Zoe thought she might burst into tears of happiness. "It's more than okay – it's amazing! Thank you so much!"

"Don't thank us," Dad said with a smile. "It was Rory's idea."

Zoe reached down to pull her little brother into a tight hug. "Thank you, Rory. You're the best brother in the world."

"Yes," Rory said, sounding very pleased with himself. "I am, aren't I?"

Zoe thought she might faint from excitement when she arrived at the elephant house after school. The camera she'd borrowed was hanging around her neck and Oliver and Max had come too, as well as her parents and Rory. Joe was waiting with a bucket of apple quarters.

"Happy birthday, Zoe," he said. "Have you had a good day?"

Zoe nodded hard. "Yes, thanks. It's about to get a million times better, though."

He smiled. "Shall we head into the enclosure, then?"

"Wait – wh-what?" Zoe stammered, blinking in astonishment. "We're going into the enclosure?"

Dad laughed. "Of course you are – how else did you think you were going to feed Saran? Her trunk won't stretch all the way up here!"

Zoe blinked hard, unable to believe her luck. "I don't know – I thought maybe I'd be helping prepare the food, not going in there to give it to her." She glanced at Oliver, who seemed to be doing his best not to look jealous. "Can Oliver come too?"

"It won't bother Saran," Joe said, shrugging. "She's used to seeing you both around now."

Oliver's face lit up as he looked at Max. "Can I, Dad?"

Max waved his hand. "Of course – if it's all right with Joe, it's okay with me."

Joe led Zoe and Oliver through the heavy gates that guarded the elephant house. Once they were inside, Joe pointed to a narrow strip of flat ground between the wall and the deep trench designed to prevent the elephants from trying to climb out.

"That's where we're going," he said, herding them towards it. "There's enough room for us all to stand safely behind the ditch – Saran can easily reach across to take the apples."

They skirted the wall until they were roughly in the centre of the thin strip. On the other side of the ditch, Saran had guessed what was happening;

she ambled towards them, holding her trunk up expectantly. She blinked at Zoe and opened her mouth in what looked like an enormous smile.

"Hello, Saran," Zoe said, hardly able to believe she was so close to the matriarch. "It's lovely to meet you."

Joe held up the bucket. "Just hold out your hand flat with the apple on your palm," he explained. "She'll do the rest."

Zoe followed his instructions and sure enough, the elephant reached over the ditch to take the apple. Zoe let out a little gurgle of pleasure as Saran's trunk grazed her palm. It felt cool and wet and a little grainy. She watched as the matriarch swung the apple into her mouth and began to chew.

Zoe reached for more fruit. This time, Saran placed her trunk on top of her head and opened her mouth wide.

"Good girl, Saran," Joe said. "This is part of our training routine, so that we can check her teeth. She's showing you how clever she is."

"You are clever," Zoe said, offering the elephant more apple. "I think you're the cleverest animal I've ever met!"

"Your turn," Zoe said to Oliver, offering him a piece of apple.

He stared at her. "No thanks. I'm not hungry."

Zoe giggled. "It's for Saran, not you! I thought you could feed her while I take some photos."

"Oh!" Oliver said, blushing and looking pleased at the same time. "Okay, thanks."

The camera clicked as Zoe snapped picture after picture, amazed all over again that they'd been allowed to get so close. After a few minutes, she put the lens cap back on the camera and she and Oliver finished feeding Saran the last of the apples.

"All gone," Zoe said, as Saran's trunk snaked towards her again. "Sorry."

Saran lifted her trunk and snorted, spraying Zoe with spit and dust. "Hey!" Zoe laughed. "That's no way to treat me on my birthday."

"Don't take it personally," Joe said, grinning. "She does it to me all the time."

The elephant seemed to feel embarrassed because she rummaged in the dust at her feet and presented Zoe with a twig.

"And now she's giving you a present, to say sorry," Joe explained. "She doesn't do that with everyone – she must really like you, Zoe."

"Thank you," Zoe said gravely, taking the twig. "I really like you too."

With a final snuffle, Saran ambled away. Joe led Zoe and Oliver along the wall, circling around the edge of the paddock to the elephant house, where there were sinks to wash their hands. It was the first time Zoe had been inside and she was amazed by how big it seemed. There were separate dens so that the elephants could be kept apart if needed, and plenty of toys, including a giant version of the boomer ball Tindu and Koko loved so much.

"It looks like you're never too big for a ball," Oliver said with a grin.

"And now it's time for the very first Savannah Safari," Dad said, when Oliver and Zoe had left the paddock and rejoined the others on the path outside. "Would you like to come too, Joe?"

Joe nodded. "Absolutely."

The start of the safari had been made to look like a ranger's station in the heart of the African savannah. It had a roof made out of thick brushwood and pillars of pale wood, with rows of benches inside and posters identifying native African species. Zoe spotted posters about poaching too, which she knew was still a major problem for many endangered species. In front of the ranger's station was a long cream-coloured open-sided bus. She recognized the man behind the steering wheel right away – it was Pete, the train driver from the Tanglewood Express.

"Happy birthday, Zoe," he called as she climbed on board. "Where shall we go today?"

Zoe grinned at Rory, waiting for him to give the answer he always gave to Pete.

"Africa," Rory said. "I want to see the gazelles!"

"You're in luck," Pete said with a grin. "There's a herd just up ahead."

He waited until everyone was settled with their seat belts fastened and then turned the key. The engine purred so softly that Zoe could hardly hear it – it was very different from the noisy clatter of the train.

"The buses run on electricity," Mum said, seeing her puzzled expression. "It's cleaner than petrol or diesel, as well as being much quieter."

The bus pulled slowly out onto the smooth road that ran between the wooden fences. A deep ditch separated the paddock from the road, with another fence beyond that, to prevent any animals from getting in or out.

Mr Fox cleared his throat. "Normally, there'll be a guide on board each bus, to give a talk and answer questions, but I'm your guide today." He pointed to a grassy paddock over to the right. "First up, we have the Thomson's gazelles. They live in large herds and can be found throughout the grasslands of Africa, particularly in the Serengeti regions and the Masai Mara National Park."

Zoe narrowed her eyes as she gazed across the paddock. "There!" she said, spotting a tall pair of antlers in the distance.

"The Thomson's gazelle is the second-fastest animal on Earth. What's the fastest, Rory?"

Rory didn't take his eyes off the paddock. "The cheetah," he said. "They can run at more than seventy miles per hour. They eat gazelles."

"When they can catch them," Dad said, his eyes crinkling into a smile. "These gazelles can manage longer distances than the cheetah and they can change direction very quickly, which can confuse the animal chasing them."

The bus was much closer to the gazelles now, near enough for Zoe to see that their horns were striped. Their fur was golden brown, with a thick diagonal strip along the side, and their legs were thin and delicate. The closest ones raised their heads as the bus rolled by and watched with obvious curiosity. Zoe lifted her camera and took a few photos.

"Coming up on the left, we have the paddock where we hope to house some endangered Rothschild's giraffes early next year," Mr Fox went on. "In the wild, they can be found in Kenya and Uganda and although they might look like other giraffes, one way to tell them apart is to look at the bottom of their legs. If it looks as though the giraffe is wearing a pair of white socks, they are Rothschild's giraffes."

Zoe exchanged a look with Oliver – she couldn't wait for the giraffes to arrive. Maybe there would be a baby in that herd too!

The bus trundled down a gentle slope and looped around the empty giraffe paddock so that they were heading back towards Tanglewood. Zoe could just about see the top of the elephant house looming in the far distance beyond a rock pile and some trees, but her attention was grabbed by Babu, who was much nearer. He was covered from head to toe in oozing brown mud from a nearby pool.

Mr Fox grinned. "As you can see, we tried to anticipate every single need our elephants might have. Here you can see Babu cooling off with a refreshing mudbath. In the savannah, a mudbath can stop an elephant from getting sunburned."

Zoe leaned towards Oliver. "That's what Raja was doing earlier, although she was using dust instead of mud."

"There's an elephant nursery in Nairobi where they cover the calves in high-factor sunscreen," Joe said. "But mud is nature's protection and it's a lot more fun."

Zoe stopped taking pictures long enough to glance over at Rory – he hated it when Mum plastered him in cream and she was sure he'd demand mud next time he was out in the sun.

"How do you clean it off?" Oliver asked.

"Some of it flakes off as it dries but we also give the elephants regular water baths," Joe explained. "As you can imagine, it takes a lot of water to give Babu a good scrub."

The road sloped upwards and the elephant house grew more and more visible over the crest of the small hill.

"That concludes today's Savannah Safari," Dad said as the bus pulled into another ranger's station to let them climb down. "I hope you enjoyed our preview visit to the African grasslands. Imagine how good it will be once the giraffes and the rhinos arrive!"

It'll be wonderful, Zoe thought as she flicked a switch on the camera and started looking through her pictures. There were some great images – she couldn't wait to print them off and stick them into her new album. The photo of Babu covered in mud was particularly great – maybe that one could go online.

Mum checked the time. "That took longer than I expected. The park is closed now but we might just squeeze in a drink at the cafe if you'd like to, Zoe?"

Zoe looked up from the camera screen and smiled.

Dolly the catering manager made excellent hot chocolate. "That would be lovely."

But when they got there, the cafe was in darkness.

"Oh, it's closed already," Zoe said, disappointed.

Mum and Dad looked at each other.

"That's strange," Mum said. "I hope everything is okay."

"We'd better go inside and make sure," Dad said, pulling open the door.

Inside, the cafe was filled with inky blackness and the serving counter was deserted. *Why isn't the door locked if there's no one here?* Zoe wondered in confusion. *What's going on?*

Suddenly, voices burst into song and a mysterious glow appeared in the dark. "Happy birthday to you, happy birthday to you!"

Dolly stepped forwards, her face lit up by the candles on a lemur-shaped birthday cake, and behind her Zoe saw lots of familiar faces. It looked as though the entire Tanglewood staff had been standing in the dark, waiting for her to arrive.

"Happy birthday, dear Zoe. Happy birthday to you!"

"Oh!" Zoe said, feeling tears prickle at the backs of her eyes. "Oh, thank you!"

"Blow out the candles," Mum said, ushering her towards Dolly. "And don't forget to make a wish!"

Everyone cheered as Zoe puffed the twelve candles out. *I wish things could be this wonderful for ever*, she thought, squeezing her eyes tight.

Then someone switched the lights on and Zoe saw the tables had been decorated with floating balloons and twirling ribbons. A banner saying *HAPPY BIRTHDAY, ZOE* hung from the ceiling. Dolly produced a tray of steaming hot chocolate to go with thick slices of sugary sweet cake.

"Better wash your hands before you see the sugar gliders again," Zoe told Shannon with a smile.

That night, Zoe gave both her parents an extra-hard hug as she went to bed. "Thank you for all my presents but most especially for letting me feed Saran."

Mum smiled. "Has it been a good birthday?"

Zoe shook her head and sighed. "Are you kidding? It's been the best birthday ever!"

Chapter Nine

Saturday dawned bright and clear. Tanglewood's keepers were at work early, making sure the animals looked their best for the bumper crowds expected for the opening of the Savannah Safari. A pair of black rhinos had arrived on Thursday and seemed to be settling in well, although they wouldn't be on display to the public for another week yet, and Zoe was certain the park's visitors would be thrilled by the new attraction. But as always at Tanglewood, there was a lot to do before the gates opened. Together with Paolo, the guinea-pig keeper, Zoe made sure Guinea Pig Central was sparkling clean. Then she hurried over to meet Oliver at the zebra enclosure, to help ensure their stripes were gleaming too. And she made sure she took plenty of pictures.

"You've definitely got the camera bug," Jenna the zebra keeper said with a grin as Zoe clicked away. "Don't forget us when you're a famous wildlife photographer!"

"No chance," Zoe said. "I want to be a zookeeper like my dad. I love animals too much to be anything else!"

The paths were definitely more crowded than usual, Zoe noticed halfway through the morning. She was delighted to see people studying the posters for the Savannah Safari – she was sure that the big photo of Dodie right in the centre was helping. *Some day it might be one of my photos up there,* Zoe thought with a squiggle of hope. The biggest crowds did seem to be outside the elephant house –

Zoe could hardly get close enough to lift her camera – but the tigers, Tindu and Koko, were popular too. So many children wanted to be a tiger or an elephant that the face-painting stand ran out of orange and grey paint. The queues for the Savannah Safari itself were long but Zoe heard lots of lovely praise as she walked through the park – it seemed everyone loved the tour, even though the attraction wasn't quite complete.

Sunday was just as busy and both Zoe and Oliver spent the day running errands for the keepers. So it wasn't until Sunday evening that Zoe found the time to go through her latest photos. She sat on the sofa in the living room and worked her way through the images, deleting the pictures where an unwitting member of the public had got in the way, or the ones that weren't quite perfect. When she reached the shots of Dodie, Zoe paused. She'd been too busy laughing at the baby elephant's antics to notice Saran in the background, but now that she wasn't distracted, Zoe could see that the matriarch's head was bowed low in every photo. She stood facing the elephant house, with her back to the herd, which was really unusual behaviour. Zoe flicked back and forth through the images, gnawing on her lip. It could be nothing...

"Dad, is everything okay with Saran?"

Her father looked up from his newspaper. "Joe says she's a bit off her food but he thinks it's because of the increase in noise and visitors over the last few days. Why do you ask?"

Zoe stood up and carried the camera over to him. "Have a look at these pictures and see what you think."

Mr Fox studied the photos carefully. By the end, his forehead was crinkled with concern.

"If you send me copies of these, I'll pass them on to Joe," he said. "But try not to worry too much – I'm sure Saran is just a little bit overwhelmed. We'll make sure she gets some peace and quiet."

"But it's half-term," Zoe pointed out. "Won't the park be busy?"

Dad smiled. "There are steps we can take to give her a break. Don't fret. And well done for spotting this – excellent work."

Normally, praise from her parents made Zoe feel good. But this time she couldn't help wishing there'd been nothing to spot.

Dad came into Zoe's room around nine-thirty on Monday morning. "Hello, sleepyhead. What are your plans for today?"

She yawned and sat up in bed. "I'm meeting Abie to show her some of my photos and I promised Shannon I'd take another picture of Hamish the sugar glider to share online before Meet the Monsters on Wednesday – the ones I took before were too dark. We're going to see how he copes with a bit more light."

He smiled. "You're doing really well with your photography. Mum and I are very pleased with the way you've thrown yourself into it."

Zoe felt a little tickle of pride. "Thanks, Dad. I'm really enjoying it."

"So, we thought you might be due a reward. How do you and Oliver fancy helping Joe to bathe Dodie today?"

Zoe gaped at him. "Really?"

"Yes, really," Dad replied. "Tembo will be there too, so that she doesn't get anxious at being kept away from her baby, but she'll have chains around her feet just in case."

Zoe bit her lip. She hated the thought of Tembo being chained up. "Does she have to?"

Dad regarded her seriously. "I'm afraid so. The chances of anything going wrong are very slim but the elephants don't know you very well yet so it's necessary. Don't worry, the chains don't hurt."

"Saran knows me," Zoe pointed out. "She gave me a present. I bet you wouldn't need to chain her up."

He hesitated. "You were absolutely right last night, Zoe. Saran isn't quite herself at the moment.

Joe is keeping an eye on her but it's best if she's kept inside for the time being."

"What's wrong with her?" Zoe asked, worry squeezing at her heart. She'd *known* something wasn't right. "Is she ill?"

Dad shook his head. "She's a bit bad-tempered, nothing a few days' rest won't fix. Now, hurry up and get dressed. We're meeting Max and Oliver at the elephant house at ten o'clock."

Zoe tried to push her anxiety about Saran out of her head and dressed as quickly as she could. She munched on a slice of toast as she walked through the park with her dad. It was busier than usual for a Monday – the half-term holiday meant plenty of visitors were still streaming through the gates, lured in by the promise of new animals and exciting exhibits. The elephant enclosure looked much emptier than normal, however; just as Mr Fox had said, Saran was inside, away from the crowds. Babu was off exploring the paddock, as usual. There was no sign of Tembo or Dodie, just Ade and Raja standing forlornly on the sandy ground.

"They look lonely," Zoe said when she saw them. "I bet they're wondering where everyone is."

"All the more reason to get on with Dodie's bath," Dad said, waving at Max and Oliver. "Then we can reunite them all."

"Aren't they worried about Saran?"

Dad shook his head. "They can manage without her for a little while and they do know where she is. Raja is the next most senior female – she can play at being the matriarch until Saran feels better."

Joe came out to meet them and led them around the side of the elephant house to a much smaller enclosure, where Dodie and Tembo were waiting. Zoe frowned at the chains around the older elephant's legs but they didn't seem to bother Tembo at all.

"Ready to get wet?" Joe said, pointing to a large, upside-down inflatable paddling pool that was leaning against the wall.

Zoe stared at the paddling pool. "She's going in there?"

"Absolutely," Joe said. He carried it over to Zoe and Oliver. "She's used to dipping in the heated pool but we use this when she's having a bath on her own – she loves it."

Oliver looked every bit as confused as Zoe felt. "Won't it burst?" he asked.

Joe handed him a hose. "It hasn't so far. But I'll change it as she grows."

"You're the expert," Oliver said, shrugging. "What do you want me to do with this?"

Joe turned on the tap in the wall. "Fill up the pool."

Once Dodie realized what was happening, she began to get excited. She dipped her trunk in the water, trying without much success to squirt it into her mouth. And she was determined to climb in before Oliver had finished filling it up. The sides bent, causing water to slop out.

"Hey!" Oliver cried, laughing at the same time. "Let me fill it up first."

Tembo watched from the side, lazily swinging

hay into her mouth. *She doesn't seem especially worried,* Zoe thought. *Maybe she's getting used to us too.*

"Okay, Oliver, I think that's enough," Joe said.

Oliver flicked the hose out of the pool and onto the floor, where it lay gushing. This time when Dodie tried to climb into the pool, she succeeded. For a moment, she stood there splashing her feet in the water. Then she lay down and rolled around, waving her legs in the air.

Zoe laughed. "She looks like a mini Babu, except less muddy!"

In a second, Dodie was back up on her feet and clambering out. Joe picked up the hose and handed it to Zoe. "Your turn. Try running the water over her back – she likes that."

Zoe did as he suggested, and the baby elephant twisted this way and that, trying to catch the gentle jet of water with her trunk.

"I wish my baths were this much fun," she said, as Dodie climbed clumsily in and out of the pool, over and over again.

"Bath time allows keepers to check their elephants for any injuries," Joe explained, keeping a close eye on Dodie. "Their skin can be surprisingly thin, so this is a good time to look for any cuts and grazes that might need treatment."

Zoe pictured the baby elephant bumbling around the enclosure – she often lost control of her legs and ended up on the ground, but one of the cows was always there to help her get back up again. In fact, the only elephant who didn't get involved with Dodie's care was her dad, Babu. Zoe found that sad, even though she knew that was exactly how it would be in the wild too, but Dodie didn't seem to mind.

"The good news is that Dodie is in perfect health," Joe went on, looking satisfied.

The water fun went on for a few more minutes until it finally seemed as though the baby elephant had had enough. She left the pool and flapped her ears hard, sending water flying in every direction.

"Thanks, Dodie," Zoe said, pulling a face as she

wiped the droplets from her eyes. "I didn't need a wash."

Once the little elephant had shaken off most of the water, she headed towards Tembo for some milk. The older elephant checked her baby over carefully with her trunk, making soft rumbling sounds that made Zoe wonder if Tembo was asking whether Dodie had enjoyed herself. Zoe was sure the baby elephant had – the swimming pool had been brilliant; just the perfect size!

"I'll take them inside now," Joe announced. "It's a bit chilly here for a wet little elephant. Thanks for your help, guys."

Oliver nodded. "Thanks for letting us help."

"Any time," Zoe said, then hesitated. "How's Saran? Dad said she's off her food."

"She is," Joe confirmed. "But she's still in good shape – I'm sure she'll bounce back in a day or two."

Zoe and Oliver exchanged a look – from what they'd seen, Saran loved her food. It really wasn't like her not to eat. *But Joe knows her best and he's not worried*, Zoe told herself. *Maybe I'm making too big a deal out of this.*

"That looked like a lot of fun," Dad said, as they made their way back to Tanglewood Manor. "I think I'd like to have a go, actually."

Zoe grinned at Oliver. "But you'd never fit in the paddling pool, Dad."

"Ha ha," Dad said, smiling. "You know exactly what I mean."

Zoe did, because it was an experience she wanted to repeat as soon as possible. Bathing Dodie was one of the coolest things she'd ever done since moving to Tanglewood – the little elephant seemed to have enjoyed it too. If only a simple bath could cheer Saran up as easily...

Chapter Ten

By Wednesday, everyone had grown worried about Saran. She'd lost interest in food completely and was getting thinner; Zoe compared the first few photos she'd taken of the elephants with the latest ones and she was sure the matriarch's skin was looking looser. That morning, Joe had let Saran out into the paddock and had caught her rubbing her cheek against one of the trees, as though something was bothering her. She'd started to snap at her family too, especially the youngest ones. Zoe felt especially sorry for Ade – Saran had roared at him for accidentally bumping into Dodie; Zoe was sure she'd heard him let out a few "woe is me" baroo rumbles afterwards.

Zoe and Oliver had been allowed to watch from the upstairs observation room in the elephant house as Max examined Saran. He took his time, checking the matriarch from head to toe, and Zoe didn't think she'd ever seen him so worried. Afterwards, they hurried down the stairs and outside to the paddock to hear his diagnosis.

"I can't be sure," Zoe overheard him say to her dad. "I don't see any problems in her mouth but I'm not an animal dentist. I might be missing something."

Zoe lowered her camera.

"Could it be…toothache?" she said hesitantly. "I know I rubbed my cheek a lot when my tooth hurt."

"We think that's very likely," Joe agreed. "But Saran is too bad-tempered to let us have a proper look in her mouth. Elephants can have problems with their teeth, particularly when they get older. I think we'd better call in an expert."

Zoe gnawed at her lip as she peered back into the elephant house and watched Saran butting a wooden pole with her tusk. The matriarch seemed like a completely different elephant to the patient, gentle animal she'd been just a few days earlier. The sooner they found out what was wrong with her, the better.

The skies had darkened by the end of the day, giving everything a shadowy and overcast feeling. The temperature had dropped too, making Zoe shiver as she headed over to the bat house for the Meet the Monsters event, and rain had started to fall. The gloomy weather matched Zoe's mood – like everyone else, she was worried about Saran. Dad had told her the dentist was arriving first thing in the morning but the matriarch's behaviour was starting to affect the herd. The cows huddled together around the younger elephants and Babu seemed especially on edge – he kept trumpeting any time something unexpected caught his eye and it was making the other elephants nervous. Zoe knew very well that unsettled elephants were much more dangerous than contented ones. She almost hoped Saran's problem *was* with her teeth – at least the animal dentist would be able to fix it, the way the human dentist had stopped Zoe's toothache. But before then, she had to focus on introducing Tanglewood's visitors to some of the park's less cute creatures. And maybe – if things went well – she'd be able to help Oliver get over his fear of spiders.

Shannon and a few of the other keepers were already inside Moonbeam Mansion when Zoe arrived. The lights were a little brighter than usual in the main hall, so that visitors would be able to see, but thick black curtains now hung over the entrance to the bat enclosure to block out the light. The keepers had arranged a tall heavy-cloth tent in front of the sugar gliders too, so that guests could stand inside and watch the creatures leap around without hurting their sensitive eyes with bright lights. At the opposite end of the hall, there were several long tables and Zoe could see a variety of glass tanks on them. She wasn't sure whether they were occupied yet but soon they would be filled with all kinds of animals – from pythons to bearded dragons and giant millipedes from other parts of the zoo. Each keeper would give a very short talk about their animals, then answer questions from the crowd.

"Any sign of Oliver yet?" Zoe asked Shannon.

The bat keeper shook her head. "No, but he definitely said he was coming. I'm sure he won't let me down."

Zoe checked her watch; guests were due to arrive for Meet the Monsters in five minutes. If Oliver didn't get a move on, he'd be late.

"I hope you've brought your camera, Zoe," Pierre the snake keeper said. "Our royal python, Queenie, just loves having her photo taken."

"Don't worry," Zoe said, smiling as she patted

the top of the camera around her neck. "I don't go anywhere without it these days."

Right at that moment, Oliver burst into the bat house. "Sorry I'm a bit late," he puffed to Shannon. "I was helping Dad give the meerkats their vaccinations."

Shannon smiled. "No problem. I'll be inside the bat enclosure most of the time but do you think you can stand outside and tell people that the bats are free-range inside? I don't want anyone to get a shock."

"Of course," Oliver said. He glanced at the tanks on the tables with an uneasy frown and turned to Zoe. "What are you going to be doing?"

"Taking pictures, mostly," she said. "Abie is coming to photograph the guests and I'm concentrating on the animals."

The sound of voices drifted through the entrance of Moonbeam Mansion.

"It sounds like the first guests are here," Shannon said. "Ready?"

Zoe and Oliver nodded.

The plastic curtain over the entrance twitched and flapped as the guests came inside.

"Welcome to Meet the Monsters," Shannon said, stepping forward. "My name is Shannon and I'm the bat keeper at Tanglewood."

The room started to fill up. Zoe was impressed at how many people there were – ticket sales had really picked up since photos of the evening's stars had gone online, and there was a good mixture of children and adults. Once it became clear that all the guests had arrived, Shannon introduced herself again.

"We called this evening Meet the Monsters but, actually, we couldn't have been further from the truth," she said. "Our spiders aren't scary, the snakes aren't slimy and our bats don't bite, unless you're a banana."

She smiled as laughter filled the room. "You're welcome to get as close to these creatures as you like, and please do ask questions. Or you can keep your distance if you'd rather but I'm pretty sure you're going to fall in love with every single one of our so-called monsters. Enjoy!"

"Show time," Zoe whispered to Oliver, as polite applause broke out among the crowd.

"This way for the fruit bats," Oliver called. "Bananas should wait outside."

The guests began to shuffle around and each keeper soon had a small audience. Zoe listened to Oliver explaining how the bat enclosure worked and then left him to it. She wanted to get as many pictures as she could.

After half an hour, the event was in full swing. The hall was filled with the sound of voices as the keepers talked and answered questions. Zoe smiled when she heard a woman exclaim how cute Charlotte the red-kneed tarantula was – that was exactly what she hoped Oliver would be saying by the end of the evening!

"How's it going?" she asked him, once he'd shown the latest group of guests into the bat enclosure.

"Great," he said. "Everyone seems to be having a good time."

Zoe held out her camera. "Want to swap?"

He took it enthusiastically. "Excellent."

"Make sure you take photos of everything," Zoe said. "Use the zoom if you don't want to get too close."

"Got it," Oliver replied, looping the strap over his head.

Zoe watched him disappear into the crowd and crossed her fingers. She'd laid the groundwork – the next part was up to Tilly, the arachnid keeper.

About ten minutes later, Zoe approached Tilly.

"Are you ready?" she said, keeping her voice low so that the group of fascinated spider fans wouldn't overhear.

"Of course," Tilly replied. "Where is he?"

Zoe glanced around and spotted Oliver taking some pictures of the python.

"He's in the photography zone," she said, trying not to grin. "All we need to do now is get him over here and 'Operation Superstar Spider' will be good to go."

Tilly winked at her. "Leave it to me."

Zoe hung back, watching as Tilly beckoned Oliver over. She watched Tilly give Oliver some instructions. He frowned and looked uncomfortable. Hiding behind an enthusiastic visitor so that Oliver wouldn't see her, Zoe held her breath. Would he do as Tilly had asked? Would he get close enough to the tarantula to take some pictures?

Oliver didn't look happy as Tilly the arachnid keeper lifted the hand that held Charlotte the tarantula towards him. Zoe saw him gulp and his hand was shaking as he lifted the camera but he didn't look directly at the spider. Instead, he kept his gaze trained on the little screen, concentrating on getting the perfect picture. The frown on his face softened a bit as he worked; Tilly continued to talk and Oliver even edged closer, angling the camera to get the best shot. He was so engrossed that he hardly seemed to notice as Charlotte stretched her hairy legs and began to walk along Tilly's arm.

"Can you turn this way please, Tilly?" he called,

still staring down at the screen. "I want to try and get her – her—"

"Her mandibles?" Tilly suggested, tickling the top of the spider's head so that she reared up and waved her front legs in the air.

Oliver grew a little bit paler and Zoe wasn't sure whether he would bolt, but instead she saw him grit his teeth and keep snapping photos. And this time he was ready when Charlotte reared up again.

"I hope you got that!" the spider keeper called.

Oliver checked the screen and then looked up at Tilly and Charlotte.

"Of course," he said, sounding relieved. "And she looks epic!"

Smiling from ear to ear, Zoe slipped into the crowd and went to find Shannon.

"Mission accomplished!" she said, high-fiving the keeper.

She glanced over to see Oliver still chatting to Tilly, who was holding Charlotte up so that he could have a closer look. As she watched, Oliver reached out a tentative finger to stroke the tarantula's hairy body.

"Wow," Zoe said, utterly delighted and amazed. "He's definitely faced up to his fear now!"

"I think you're right," Shannon said with an impressed nod. "Well done, Zoe, your plan worked like a dream."

Zoe blushed modestly. "It's Oliver who deserves the praise. And Charlotte!"

Zoe awoke to the sound of rain rattling against her window. Downstairs in the kitchen, her parents were discussing Saran's appointment with the elephant dentist.

"Max wants her to wear chains and I agree," Dad said.

"Does she have to?" Zoe objected in dismay.

"She's obviously in pain," Dad replied. "And that makes her unpredictable. It's safest for everyone this way."

I suppose it makes sense, Zoe decided reluctantly. It was vital that they found out exactly what was wrong with the matriarch, after all. "Okay. Can I—?"

"I know what you're going to ask, Zoe," Dad cut in, "and the answer is no. You can't be there when the dentist sees her."

"Ben," Mum said, as Zoe's face fell.

Dad's expression softened. "I know you're worried. But I promise I'll pass on any news as soon as I can."

Zoe found it difficult to focus on her duties that morning. She had to concentrate extra hard on everything, double-checking to make sure she'd filled all the guinea pigs' water bottles and locked the enclosures once she'd finished. She checked her watch, wondering whether the dentist had been yet. Dad had said she couldn't be in the elephant house when he examined Saran but there was nothing to stop her from watching the other elephants from outside the enclosure, was there?

It was still raining as she walked through the

park, meaning that there weren't as many visitors around. Zoe pulled the hood of her coat up around her ears – the grey day matched her mood somehow, and not even the majestic sight of the new black rhino pair, grazing in their enclosure, could cheer her up completely. She hoped she'd feel better once the dentist knew what was wrong with Saran.

It was obvious that the other elephants were missing Saran too. Raja was doing her best to fill the gap, but Tembo and Ade both stood with their heads down, trunks trailing along the wet sandy floor. There was no sign of Babu. The only bright spot was Dodie, who was trying to nudge a ball around the enclosure with her trunk and trumpeting loudly when it didn't roll the way she wanted.

Oliver arrived around ten minutes after Zoe.

"Any news?" he asked, with an anxious glance at the closed doors of the elephant house.

Zoe shook her head. "No."

"I hope it isn't serious," Oliver said. "Dad says that when an elderly elephant has a tooth problem in the wild, it can mean trouble. Sometimes they die."

"Don't say that!" Zoe said, her eyes filling with tears. "I'm sure the dentist will be able to fix it."

Oliver looked as though he was sorry. "Yeah." He watched Dodie playing for a moment and his face brightened. "Hey, can you send me the photo you took of me holding Charlotte?"

Zoe nodded. Just before the end of the Meet the Monsters event, Tilly had persuaded Oliver to hold Charlotte in his hand and Zoe had been right there with the camera. "Of course," she told him. "It's an amazing shot – you look so proud of yourself."

"I was," he said, sounding pleased. "I've been scared of spiders all my life but the weird thing was that by the end of the evening, Charlotte didn't bother me."

Zoe tried her hardest not to smile. "Good."

"Listen," Oliver said. "My dad says there's an animal photography competition running at the moment – you should enter."

"Really?" Zoe said. "That sounds like fun. I've got plenty of photos to choose from—"

She stopped mid-sentence as the door of the elephant house opened and Max, Mr Fox and the dentist appeared.

She exchanged an agonized look with Oliver and they both ran towards the gates.

The three men were deep in conversation when Zoe and Oliver skidded to a halt in front of them. Dad gave them a sad smile. "It's not good news. I'm afraid Saran has an infected tooth – that's why she'd stopped eating. Joe's with her now – she's going to need to have it removed."

Zoe blinked, remembering how the dentist had fixed her own tooth. She'd had to stay very still and that was only to fix a tiny hole – it wasn't very likely that Saran would let the animal dentist remove a whole tooth. "So she'll need to be asleep?"

Max nodded. "Yes, we'll need to anaesthetize her while the operation is performed and that's always risky with an elderly animal. But we don't have any choice

– she's lost a lot of weight and her health is suffering."

The dentist gave Zoe and Oliver a reassuring smile. "Don't worry – Saran is in safe hands. My name is Andrew and I fly all over the world looking after my animal patients. I've never lost one yet."

"We'll get the elephant house ready," Max said. "Are you free to operate on Saran first thing tomorrow morning?"

Andrew nodded. "The sooner we get started, the sooner we'll have Saran up on her feet and back to normal."

Zoe and Oliver exchanged worried looks.

"I hope he's right," Oliver mumbled as the three adults walked away.

"Saran's a fighter," Zoe said, clenching her fists with determination. "She'll pull through."

She glanced across at Raja and Ade, who were still standing in the rain, their trunks drooping with misery. *Please get better, Saran,* Zoe thought fretfully, wishing the elderly elephant could hear her. *Your family really needs you.*

Chapter Eleven

Friday morning was cold and wet.

Rain drummed against the windows of Tanglewood HQ, the control room that housed all the security screens around the park. From there, under the supervision of Ruth the security guard, Zoe and Oliver were allowed to watch the camera feed from the elephant house as Saran was anaesthetized. Clenching her hands so hard that her fingers turned white, Zoe stared at the screen as the matriarch dropped first to her knees and then onto her side on the floor of the elephant house, which had been covered with special antibacterial sheets. Seconds ticked by and became minutes; Zoe and Oliver looked at each other nervously. How long did it take for an elephant to fall deeply enough asleep for an operation?

"What if she doesn't wake up again?" Zoe whispered fearfully.

"She will," Oliver said, but he looked worried and Zoe knew he was thinking of Saran's age and her weakness from not eating. "She's going to be just fine."

After what felt like an age, the dentist turned to Max and gave him a thumbs-up gesture.

"Okay, that's enough," Ruth said firmly. "Your mum said there's no way you're watching the operation, Zoe."

Oliver went home, leaving Zoe alone with her mother and little brother. Time passed so slowly that she was certain her watch must have stopped.

Outside, the rain continued to fall and she tried to bury herself in her much-neglected homework, but she couldn't help sneaking glances at the time. Lunchtime came and went without any news from the elephant house and by the time one o'clock rolled around, Zoe couldn't bear it any longer.

"Can't I go into the park?" she begged Mum for what felt like the hundredth time. "I promise not to make any noise."

Mrs Fox pursed her lips. "You know what Dad said – you and Oliver are to keep away until he gives the all-clear. And if that takes all day then so be it."

"What about me?" Rory asked, looking up from his zoo animals. "Am I allowed to go in?"

"I'm afraid not," Mum said, with a gentle shake of her head. "Daddy and Max want things to be as quiet as possible."

"But—" Zoe tried again.

"No, Zoe," Mum said firmly. "Don't ask me again."

By mid-afternoon, Zoe was so restless that she thought she might explode. She tried not to think about how Saran's operation was going but it was hard. Was the total lack of news a good thing? Or did it mean there was a problem?

"Are you sure your phone isn't broken?" she asked Mum eventually.

Mum glanced at the handset. "It's fine. Try to be patient – Dad will let us know as soon as there's any news."

Zoe pushed her schoolbooks across the kitchen table. "Can I go over and see Oliver instead? I bet he's worried too."

Just then, there was a knock at the manor's oak front door. Zoe jumped up and ran to answer it.

"Oliver!" she exclaimed when she saw him panting on the doorstep, his hair wet and shining from the rain. Her heart thudded in her chest as she stared at him. "What is it?"

"Good news," he puffed. "Dad says the operation was a complete success. They removed the tooth and treated the infection – Saran is awake and on her feet!"

"Woo hoo!" Zoe crowed, delight coursing through her. "Yay for Saran!"

Mum and Rory appeared in the hallway behind her. "That's excellent news," Mum said. "I've just had a message to say the same thing."

Zoe turned to Mum. "*Now* can we go into the park?"

Mum checked her phone and nodded. "Dad says you have to be quiet."

"We will!" Zoe said, reaching for her wellies. "Honestly, he won't even know that we're there."

Rain dripped from the trees as Zoe and Oliver hurried towards the elephant house. "What a horrible day," Oliver said, glancing up at the lead-coloured skies. "No wonder all the visitors have stayed at home."

It was true, Zoe thought as she pulled her scarf up around her neck to keep out the chill, the park was almost deserted. Even the keen amateur photographers who could usually be found hanging around outside the big-cat enclosures had gone. Zoe could hardly blame them – Tanglewood was freezing cold, and thoroughly damp and unpleasant. It almost felt as if winter had come early.

The elephants look worried and miserable too, Zoe thought as she got nearer. Raja and Tembo were huddling together next to the wall of the elephant house, comforting each other with gentle sniffs and touches, and Ade was trotting back and forth across the paddock, looking anxious. They're scared, Zoe thought, wondering how she'd feel if her own mum needed an operation – distracted and afraid, probably. Zoe wished she could give the elephants a hug and tell them everything was okay, but she supposed the only thing that would make them feel better was seeing Saran safe and well again. As Zoe watched, Ade raised his trunk and let out a shrill, forlorn-sounding trumpet. They were all lost without their matriarch.

"Not long now," Zoe whispered. "You'll see her soon."

"Zoe," Oliver said, in a strange-sounding voice, "where's Dodie?"

Frowning, Zoe peered around Tembo's legs. "She must be there. Is she hiding behind Raja?"

Oliver began to walk faster. "I can't see her. Maybe she's down by the ditch."

Zoe followed him to the wall and, together, they stared downwards. Dodie was not there.

Oliver pulled his phone from his pocket. "She's not in the paddock. I'm going to phone Dad."

He tapped at the screen and Zoe strained her eyes as she stared towards the unfenced fields beyond the sandy paddock, the ones that stretched out of sight. Surely the little elephant couldn't have gone exploring on her own?

"Dad, listen," Oliver said into his phone. "You haven't got Dodie inside the elephant house, have you?" He stopped talking. "Has Joe taken her to the small enclosure for a bath?"

Zoe watched Oliver's face become more and more worried. He covered the handset with his hand.

"Dad says they haven't got her. He says she was out here with Tembo and Raja."

Zoe felt all the colour drain from her face as she realized what that meant. Wherever Dodie was, she was on her own. Maybe that's why Ade had trumpeted – he wasn't calling to Saran: he was calling to his sister.

Oliver uncovered the phone. "She's not out here, Dad," he said, his voice strained and urgent. "Dodie is missing."

By the time they'd checked every inch of the enclosure and the elephant house to make certain the baby elephant wasn't hiding anywhere, the sky had grown darker.

Joe glanced around, an anxious look on his face. "We need to start searching the fields for her right now. It's too cold for her to be outside after nightfall – she could die if her core temperature drops too low."

Zoe's dad shook his head.

"Someone needs to stay with Saran, Joe," he said,

his breath clouding in the cold evening air. "You're the person she trusts the most."

For a second, Zoe thought the keeper would argue with her dad. Then Joe ran his hand through his hair and sighed. "You're right. But you'll need to be careful if you're searching the fields on foot. Babu is still out there and I don't need to remind you how dangerous bull elephants can be if they feel threatened."

Mr Fox nodded. "Okay, Max and I can round up a couple of the other keepers and we'll start looking. We're going to need torches."

"I want to help," Zoe said, stepping forward. "Oliver and I are good at finding lost animals – we'll come too."

"Not this time," Dad replied. "You heard Joe, it's much too dangerous."

"But we found Flash when he was lost," Zoe insisted. "And Dodie knows Oliver and me."

"Babu doesn't," Dad said, his tone final. "I mean it, Zoe. You and Oliver need to go back home and wait."

He turned his back on Zoe, signalling the

conversation was over. She stared at him, tears of frustration and fear brimming at her eyes. Oliver tugged at her arm. "Come on, Zoe. Let's go."

Zoe couldn't help it; she cried as she walked away. Joe was right – Dodie was far too young to survive out in the cold fields alone. What if they didn't get to her before it got dark?

"I'm sure they'll find her," Oliver said, but he didn't sound as though he believed it. Zoe thought back to their ride on the Savannah Safari bus and the wide expanse of land with rock piles and trees. "Mum designed it to be as much like the savannah as possible, to give the herd plenty of space to roam. And Dodie only has little legs," she said, as they passed the ranger's station, with its cream-coloured bus parked outside. "I'm scared."

Pete poked his head around the side of the bus. "Hey now, what's up?"

His expression grew grave as Zoe and Oliver explained. "And they think she's somewhere out in the field?"

"Where else could she be?" Oliver said. "But there's a lot of ground to cover and it's freezing now."

Pete thought for a second, then his face brightened.

"Hop on board," he said, waving a hand at the bus. "You can look for Dodie from the safety of these seats."

"Can we?" Zoe gasped. "Oh, Pete, that would be brilliant!"

Oliver didn't look sure. "I don't know," he said in a low voice only Zoe could hear. "We're supposed to go home."

But Zoe was already heading towards the creamy door. "We'll be perfectly safe. Come on, Oliver – we don't have time to waste!"

The sky was starting to turn an inky blue as Pete drove past the gazelles. Zoe squinted into the half-light; pretty soon it would be too dark to see.

"Can't you go any faster?" she begged Pete.

"No can do," he called back. "This thing was built to save the planet, not break the speed limit."

Zoe sat back, shivering a little as she fiddled with the lens cap of her camera. Oliver seemed just as tense – he kept peering out of the window, even though they had only just reached the empty giraffe enclosure.

"Come on," Oliver muttered, staring at the gloomy sky.

The bus began to dip as it approached the elephant paddock and both Oliver and Zoe dashed to the side of the bus nearest to it, their seat belts forgotten.

"There's Babu!" Oliver shouted, pointing at the hulking bull elephant in the distance. "But I can't see Dodie."

Zoe peered into the shadows, desperately searching for any sign of the calf. "Is she behind him?"

Oliver stared for a long moment, then slumped into his seat. "No. She's not there."

Zoe kept her gaze trained on the fields, silently wishing the bus would move faster. She gave her phone a swift glance, hoping to see a message to say the missing baby had been found, but the screen was blank. Her stomach somersaulted with nerves as the bus purred onwards.

"It's going to be so much harder to search in the dark," she said with a distressed glance at Oliver.

It's so different from the last time we made this journey, Zoe thought, trying to calm her nerves. *I took that amazing photo of Babu after he'd been wallowing in that mud hole. I bet it's more like a mud river today…*

"That's it!" she gasped. "I know where Dodie is!"

Oliver stared at her. "Where?"

"In the mud hole," Zoe gabbled. "It's rained so much that I bet she wouldn't be able to resist it. Oh, please hurry up, Pete!"

The driver threw her a determined look. "Fasten your seat belts. I'll see what I can do."

The bus sped up, lurching forwards as though it ran on rocket fuel instead of electricity. Zoe craned her neck to see the mud hole. She let out a strangled shout when it came into view. "There! I can see her – she's there!"

The top of the baby elephant was clearly in view – her trunk was waving and the sound of faint trumpeting filled the air. But her bottom half seemed to be submerged in the ground.

"It's the mud," Oliver cried. "She must be stuck!"

He pulled out his phone and stabbed at the screen. "Dad, we've found her! Dodie is stuck in the mud hole right at the bottom of the slope."

He listened impatiently to the tinny voice on the other end of the phone, then interrupted. "No, we're on the bus with Pete. Just hurry up, Dad – she sounds scared and tired!"

Chapter Twelve

Pete stopped the bus as soon as it was alongside Dodie.

Zoe jumped up. "Open the doors!"

The driver shook his head. "No, it's not safe. We'll wait here until the others arrive."

Zoe sat down again, feeling her eyes prickle with helpless tears. Dodie's cries seemed weaker now – was Oliver right? Was the baby elephant running out of strength? She trained her gaze on the top of the slope, willing her dad to arrive. He'd know what to do, she was sure of it.

"Look!" Oliver said, pointing up the hill. "There's something moving. It must be them."

Zoe peered into the half-light, relief flooding through her. Then she frowned – the figure was the wrong shape to be a human. It was too big and there seemed to be two wide flaps either side…

"Babu!" she shouted joyfully. "He must have heard Dodie crying."

The bull elephant trundled down the slope towards the baby, his ears flapping as he walked.

"Will he know what to do?" Oliver asked. "I don't think I've ever seen him even look at Dodie before."

Zoe clenched her fists. "He'll know. Elephants are smart, even the bulls."

Oliver threw her a sideways look. "I know it's usually the cows who take care of the young, but dads can be pretty cool too."

Zoe felt her face turn red; he meant Max, who

had looked after him alone after Oliver's mother had died a few years earlier.

"Yeah, I know," she said, managing a lopsided smile. "Sorry."

Dodie's struggles increased when she saw her father and her cries grew more frantic. Babu stopped at the edge of the mud, as though working out the best way to reach her, and then he stepped forwards and touched his daughter's head with his trunk. He let out a gentle soothing rumble as he stroked her, and almost immediately her struggles became less panicky. The rumbling went on, changing in tone until it seemed to Zoe to become almost encouraging. Dodie began to push with her legs again and Babu curled his long trunk around her body and gently pulled upwards. There was a loud squelch as the mud sucked at Dodie. Babu rumbled at her again and she pushed once more, forcing herself upwards. The bull elephant raised his head, heaving the baby out of the mud. And with a loud squelch, Dodie was free.

"Yes!" Zoe cried, punching the air in delight.

Oliver closed his eyes for a moment. "Well done, Babu."

The bull elephant guided Dodie to the edge of the mud, where she promptly sat down. Babu flicked his trunk over her, as though making sure she was unhurt, and she raised her own trunk to touch his.

"Aw," Zoe said, beaming. "They're so sweet together."

Her attention was caught by sudden flickering lights at the top of the hill. "It's Dad," Zoe said, her stomach tightening. "We need to warn them not to scare Babu!"

Oliver lifted his phone to his ear. "Way ahead of you," he said. "Dad? Dodie is okay. Babu saved her."

The torches went out abruptly and Zoe turned back to the elephants. Babu was still talking to her, his low grumbling roar rolling over the baby elephant's head as he nudged her with his trunk. Dodie seemed to listen and, with his help, she managed to stand up. Babu then began to walk slowly towards home, his trunk never leaving his daughter's side.

Oliver had noticed too. His eyes widened.

"I think maybe you should back off, Dad," he said into his phone. "It looks like Babu has got everything under control."

Zoe watched as the bull elephant helped Dodie climb the hill. Then she turned to Pete. "I think our work here is done. Let's go home."

Pete tipped his driver's cap and smiled. "Right you are, Zoe. The safari's over."

Zoe and Oliver jumped from the bus almost before it had stopped and ran at full speed towards the elephant enclosure. They joined Max and Zoe's dad just in time to see Tembo spot Babu and hurry towards them, flapping her ears hard and letting out the loudest rumble Zoe had ever heard. She reached down and brushed Dodie's head tenderly, then touched trunks with Babu, as though thanking him. Raja arrived next and Ade was right behind her, rumbling out a greeting of his own. He charged towards Babu, clanking his small tusks against the bull elephant's larger ones in a joyous hello, and then spun round in a surprisingly graceful circle.

"Woah!" Oliver said, laughing. "It looks like Ade could teach Kushpu a move or two!"

"Aren't they amazing?" Zoe's dad said, glancing down at her. "They might have given me a few more grey hairs today but I'm so glad they came to Tanglewood."

The elephant family walked into the enclosure, each of them taking a moment to greet Dodie with their trunk. Raja brushed trunks with Babu too – it was all so lovely and touching that Zoe felt she might burst with happiness as she took picture after picture. And then she noticed the door of the elephant house was opening, filling the enclosure with light. Joe poked his head through the gap.

"Room for one more?" he called.

He stepped out of the way and Saran's majestic head appeared. The other elephants let out a roar of greeting and trotted to greet the matriarch. They fussed over her, letting out soft, cooing rumbles as though they were telling her they'd missed her. And then Saran seemed to notice her mud-covered granddaughter and spent a moment investigating.

"She's asking what on earth has been going on," Zoe said, snapping more photos and grinning at Oliver.

"You're probably right," Oliver agreed. "It's funny the way we can almost understand them but not quite."

Saran flapped her ears and turned back towards the warmth of the elephant house.

"And now she's telling them it's time to come in out of the cold," Zoe said. "Just like a grandmother would."

They watched as the herd followed Saran inside. Joe closed the doors behind them.

"I think we'll leave them in peace for a little while," Max said to Zoe's dad. "I'd like to check little Dodie over this evening, just to make sure she's not hurt, but she looks as though she's in safe hands."

"Good idea," Mr Fox said. "I think we've all had enough excitement for one day, don't you?"

He glanced at Zoe and Oliver as he spoke, and Zoe wondered whether he was going to tell them off for disobeying him. But he smiled instead. "Well done, you two. I know I should be angry that you didn't do as you were told, but you did find Dodie."

Zoe shook her head.

"No, Babu found Dodie," she said. "You should have seen how gentle and careful he was with her."

"Even so, I think you deserve a reward," Dad said. "I'll have a word with Mum and see if we can come up with a special treat for the two of you."

"Thanks, Dad," Zoe said, holding out one hand to high-five Oliver.

A shout rang out from the enclosure. Zoe looked down to see Joe waving up at them. "Hey, Zoe and Oliver," he called. "I don't suppose you can help me to solve another elephant emergency, can you?"

Zoe looked at Oliver in alarm. What now?

"Of course," Oliver called, sounding worried. "What do you need us to do?"

Joe smiled. "I've got a very muddy little baby here and I think she'd love you to give her a nice warm bath!"

Zoe burst out laughing. "Now that's the kind of elephant emergency I like!"

The End

Everybody's Talking About
TANGLEWOOD ANIMAL PARK!

"This is a roarsome book! I love it! 1000 out of 10!" Finley ☺, aged 8

"Outstandingly gripping"
Daniel, aged 8

"I did not want to put it down because I did not want the fun to end."
Dior, aged 8

"I love reading about all of the animals. The book makes me want to go and visit Tanglewood."
Freya, aged 6

"I really loved reading this book, 10/10." Holly, aged 9

"This is a roarsome book! I love it!

"I just could not take my eyes off this book. It reminds me so much about myself and my love for animals, just like Zoe!"
Lila, aged 10

"I think this book is the best book I have ever read" Ava, aged 6

"This book was amazingly cool!!!" Ridha, aged 8

"I'd love to live with the main character Zoe. I will be telling all my friends to read this book."
Charlotte, aged 9

"When I read about Flash the zebra being born it made me feel emotional."
Leila, aged 8

"I wish I lived in Tanglewood like Zoe. This book was amazingly cool!!!"

Catch up with Zoe's adventures at Tanglewood Animal Park!

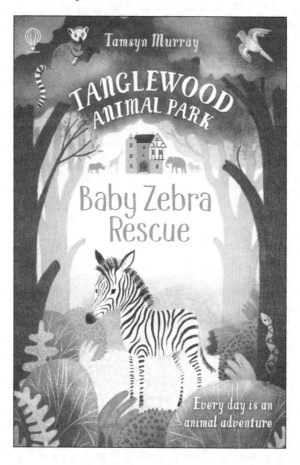

Zoe loves living at Tanglewood Animal Park and taking care of the animals. She splashes with penguins, feeds the lemurs - she even sees baby zebra, Flash, being born. It's a dream come true.

Then Flash goes missing. Now Zoe has to find him, and soon! Where can that baby zebra be?

ISBN: 9781474903035

OUT NOW!

Zoe can't wait to meet the park's newest arrival,
Tindu the tiger. But Tindu seems sad,
and refuses to leave his den.

Can Zoe dream up a plan to help
Tanglewood's tiger feel happy
in his new home?

ISBN: 9781474903042

Acknowledgements

Enormous thanks to everyone at Paradise Wildlife Park for supporting Tanglewood – in particular, Lynn Whitnall, Ian Jones and Cassie Woods. At Colchester Zoo, I must thank Clive Barwick and Claire Bennett for sharing their elephant expertise and letting me meet their gorgeous matriarch. Any mistakes are absolutely down to me.

Much love Special Agent Jo Williamson – I couldn't do this without you.

At Usborne, I owe a huge debt of gratitude to Team Tanglewood: my wonderful editor, Stephanie King, for her patience and grace when dealing with a difficult author and to Jenny Tyler, Rebecca Hill, Anne Finnis, Sarah Stewart and Becky Walker for ensuring Tanglewood shines. To Stevie Hopwood and

Sarah Connell for working their PR and marketing magic. Thanks also to Hannah Cobley and Amy Manning for designing the cover and Sarah Cronin and Hannah Cobley for designing the inside of the book so gorgeously.

Special thanks to Jean Claude, Courtesy of Advocate Art, and Chuck Groenink for their illustrations.

I owe a lot to the amazing Elaine Penrose – thanks for supporting me and my books!

And lastly, thanks to my lovely children, T and E, who continue to allow me to visit zoos while pretending it is all for their benefit.

Usborne Quicklinks

For links to websites where you can watch video clips about lots of different animals, find out about the life of zookeepers and test your animal know-how with quizzes, games and activities, go to the Usborne Quicklinks website at www.usborne.com/quicklinks and enter the keywords "Elephant Emergency".

When using the internet, please make sure you follow our three basic rules:
• Always ask an adult's permission before using the internet.
• Never give out personal information, such as your name, address, the name of your school or telephone number.
• If a website asks you to type in your name or email address, check with an adult first.

To find out more about internet safety, go to the Help and advice page at the Usborne Quicklinks website. We recommend that children are supervised while using the internet.